## Bolan needed answers, any way he could get them

He unleathered the Desert Eagle, but just as he got off a shot, autofire rang out, shredding the tree bark next to his head. He threw himself against the slender aspen as bullets raked the trail, then chanced a look around the corner. Peterson and another Right Hand of God hardman were crouched behind the trees in the distance. Bolan triggered the Desert Eagle three times, drilling .44 slugs into Peterson's tree cover.

The Executioner scanned the area for their Jeep, hoping to disable the vehicle, then move in on the ex-lawmen. He saw he wasn't going to get the chance to take the fight to the enemy. Firing wildly with their assault rifles, they forced him to stay under cover as rounds tore at the tree bark.

He waited for a lull in the firing to move out. It came a second later when he heard the vehicle's engine roar to life. Sliding out onto the trail, Bolan watched as a dust cloud rose in the distance. Then the rev of the engine pealed over the clearing before slowly fading.

The war in the town of Honor had begun. Bolan knew he was at the top of the Right Hand of God's list of targets.

# MACK BOLAN ®

## The Executioner

# DON PENDLETON'S
# THE EXECUTIONER®
## DEATH FORCE

# A GOLD EAGLE BOOK FROM
# WORLDWIDE®

TORONTO • NEW YORK • LONDON
AMSTERDAM • PARIS • SYDNEY • HAMBURG
STOCKHOLM • ATHENS • TOKYO • MILAN
MADRID • WARSAW • BUDAPEST • AUCKLAND

First edition December 1996
ISBN 0-373-64216-4

Special thanks and acknowledgment to
Dan Schmidt for his contribution to this work.

DEATH FORCE

The distinction between private violence and public force is the central principle of a civilized society.

—Walter Lippmann

Immoral men can't claim that they are fighting to save the world from losing all sense of morality. Noble sentiments like that are meaningless when they come from those who have no sense of honor.

—Mack Bolan

# THE
# MACK BOLAN®
## LEGEND

Nothing less than a war could have fashioned the destiny of the man called Mack Bolan. Bolan earned the Executioner title in the jungle hell of Vietnam.

But this soldier also wore another name—Sergeant Mercy. He was so tagged because of the compassion he showed to wounded comrades-in-arms and Vietnamese civilians.

Mack Bolan's second tour of duty ended prematurely when he was given emergency leave to return home and bury his family, victims of the Mob. Then he declared a one-man war against the Mafia.

He confronted the Families head-on from coast to coast, and soon a hope of victory began to appear. But Bolan had broken society's every rule. That same society started gunning for this elusive warrior—to no avail.

So Bolan was offered amnesty to work within the system against terrorism. This time, as an employee of Uncle Sam, Bolan became Colonel John Phoenix. With a command center at Stony Man Farm in Virginia, he and his new allies—Able Team and Phoenix Force—waged relentless war on a new adversary: the KGB.

But when his one true love, April Rose, died at the hands of the Soviet terror machine, Bolan severed all ties with Establishment authority.

Now, after a lengthy lone-wolf struggle and much soul-searching, the Executioner has agreed to enter an "arm's-length" alliance with his government once more, reserving the right to pursue personal missions in his Everlasting War.

**1**

Mack Bolan, a.k.a. the Executioner, knew death was coming down hard and furious on the lawman. At first, it had looked like a routine traffic stop, but the ordinary had turned deadly in the blink of an eye. With the worst-case scenario for any lawman under way, Bolan could only take it to the enemy with guns blazing. He might be too late to save Colorado's finest, but at least he could throw it back into the face of unknown gunmen.

The muzzle-flashes and relentless chatter of automatic weapons thrust Bolan into full combat alert. The pencil-tip flames of those weapons stabbed the night along the deserted stretch of Rocky Mountain highway, some fifty yards dead ahead, and the Executioner saw the state trooper tumble to the road under a screaming rain of bullets and flying glass.

The Executioner's proposed R and R had suddenly slammed into a bloody dead end.

Racing his Ford Bronco toward the cruiser, Bolan hit his high beams long enough to take in the scene. He reached inside his black leather bomber jacket, coming out with the big .44 Magnum Desert Eagle holstered there in a shoulder rig. The Executioner counted three men armed with M-16 assault rifles—two on the passenger's side of a black van and one gunman near the rear of the driver's side.

For a moment the trio of gunmen was bathed in the glare of Bolan's high beams and the cruiser's rotating cherry. The Executioner caught the steely glare of eyes that warned him he was dealing with pros and stone killers.

With the fallen trooper slumped beside the open door of his cruiser, his chest wet with blood, Bolan knew he was the next target. He hit the brakes, sending the Bronco into a long sliding squeal of rubber. He then whipped the wheel hard to the right, throwing the passenger side at the gunmen in a maneuver meant to shield the downed trooper from taking any more hits. If the lawman was still breathing, then Bolan intended to make sure he stayed alive.

Just as he had anticipated, the enemy cut loose with their assault rifles, and the Bronco's windshield and passenger window exploded in a sea of flying glass. Bolan burst out the door, the Desert Eagle in hand. He moved to the back of the vehicle as the thundering hellstorm of 5.56 mm lead pounded the truck for several moments.

Then the gunfire ceased, and Bolan heard the enemy cracking home fresh clips. He used the lull to find the trooper. He lay in a growing pool of blood on a bed of glass slivers, making a sound somewhere between a gasp and a gurgle. Bolan knew the man had taken one through the lung. With blood pouring from the trooper's mouth and his face drained of color, Bolan knew that if he didn't get the man help, he would die within minutes. Suddenly the soldier heard the voice of a male dispatcher come over the radio inside the cruiser, demanding that Trooper Cowlins respond.

Then the rap of hard-soled shoes on asphalt snagged Bolan's attention. They were coming straight at him. He knew they had the heavier firepower, so he wasn't counting on being able to take the trio out with the Desert Eagle. But he could make at least one or two of them regret this night forever, possibly shoot out their tires if they tried to run for it.

Bolan gauged the distance between the van and himself—twenty yards, about the same length as between the cruiser and the van. Bolan had no idea why the trooper had stopped the vehicle, but the gunmen most certainly had something to hide, something over which they would murder. With the dispatcher demanding a response from the trooper, the Executioner suspected the location was marked. He hoped that, in the event the gunmen managed to flee, the trooper had already given the dispatcher a description of the van and license number, because he was certain he wasn't about to get a good look at the plates.

Bolan popped up, drawing instant target acquisition on one of the two gunmen moving toward him from the van's passenger side. The soldier triggered the hand cannon and dropped one of the hardmen with a slug that caught him high in the chest and kicked him off his feet. When the guy kept screaming in agony for long moments, Bolan knew he hadn't taken him out for good. No sooner did the peal of thunder from the Desert Eagle roll over the highway than Bolan came under relentless autofire. He was forced to duck, as a tidal wave of glass blew over his head and slugs sparked and whined off the asphalt around the Bronco. Bolan realized he had to get the trooper out of the line of fire. He reached the cruiser's open door, and with his return fire saw that he had the gunmen engaged in a fighting retreat for the van.

The guy Bolan had dropped kept crying in pain as he was dragged along by his comrade, who fired his M-16 one-handed. The other gunman kept pouring it on with his own flaming assault rifle. The hellstorm of lead continued to slam the Bronco, then tracked on for the cruiser, the windshield obliterated in the next instant by a barrage of autofire. There was no chance, Bolan knew, of getting off a clear shot at the van's tires.

As the headlights on the cruiser burst under the rain of lead, Bolan pulled the trooper to the back of his vehicle. Then, sliding around to the passenger's side, the soldier reached the door and managed to open it. The assault rifles continued to hammer the cruiser, and Bolan hit the seat on his side, glass crunching beneath him and digging into his jacket. He grabbed the mike and shouted, "You've got an officer down."

"What the hell is going on? Who are you?" the dispatcher demanded.

"I'm the guy who's trying to save your trooper," Bolan yelled over the barrage of 5.56 mm slugs that whined off the cruiser. The rearview mirror exploded over Bolan's head. "You'd better get a Medevac chopper here ASAP, or this trooper's not going to make it." Bolan heard a door slam. He looked up through the jagged teeth of the battered windshield, then ducked as another hurricane of lead began to assault the cruiser. "Three suspects, male Caucasian, one of them's shot. They're driving a black van, but I can't see the plates. Is this call marked?"

"I know where you are. Backup is on the way."

Bolan heard the van's engine roar to life and knew he was about to lose the gunmen. "Get some units north of this position. I just passed a sign, about five miles back, that said I'm in Honor County. Highway 69. You copy?"

"I said I know where you are!"

Bolan let the mike go and slid out of the cruiser. It was then that the whiff of gasoline from the vehicle's tank hit him. One wild shot, and he and the trooper would be consumed in an explosion. The Executioner raced to the lawman and threw him over his shoulder in a fireman's carry. He heard the gunning of an engine, and as the van sluiced out onto the highway, Bolan saw the gunman, holding on to the doorjamb, still triggering his M-16 with his free hand.

Just as Bolan had feared, a line of slugs began to stitch the cruiser before sparking off the gas-soaked asphalt. As the soldier ran down the road's shoulder, veering for the woods, flames whooshed to life beneath the cruiser. A moment later, the vehicle was sheared apart by an ear-shattering explosion that turned the area behind Bolan into a roiling wall of flames. Twisted wreckage spun across the highway, and the force of the blast knocked Bolan to the ground, throwing the lawman from his shoulder.

With the mushrooming fireball lighting the dark road, momentarily turning night into day around the kill zone, Bolan could only watch as the van's wheelman gunned the engine again, flooring the vehicle. Moments later, the van was swallowed up by the night.

Then, except for crackling flames, there was silence.

Suddenly Trooper Cowlins groaned and hacked up blood. Bolan knelt by the lawman.

"Easy, Cowlins. Hold on, help is on the way."

As if realizing he was only a few moments away from death, Cowlins grabbed Bolan by the arm in a viselike grip. He opened his mouth, struggling to say something, but nothing but blood came out.

"Stay still," Bolan said, gently forcing the trooper to lay back. He shrugged off his jacket and placed it over the lawman. The Executioner was about to check his wounds when Cowlins convulsed violently, then let out a long death rattle. Just like that, it was over. He brushed the man's eyes shut.

Where the hell was backup? Bolan wondered, searching the highway to the south. There was nothing but silence and flames, and a dead cop.

A delayed blast belched from the cruiser's wreckage.

Bolan stood. He was about to check the Bronco, intending to go after the killers, when he saw flashing lights, racing straight at him from the south. He counted six cruisers.

He'd expected at least two or three of the units to go roaring past him in pursuit of the van. Instead, all six went into long squealing slides, two of the vehicles screeching to a halt by the fiery wreckage. Moments later the Executioner found himself staring down nearly a dozen enraged state troopers with 9 mm pistols or shotguns drawn and pointed at him.

"Get your hands up! On the ground! Now!" a voice bellowed from the darkness.

Several troopers jacked the actions on their 12-gauge riot guns.

Bolan clenched his jaw, slowly raising his arms.

"I told you to get on the ground! Face-down!"

The soldier understood their rage and suspicion, but he didn't like it, especially not when the killers were getting away. He hesitated.

"If you don't get on the ground now, mister, we'll drop you where you stand!"

Bolan cursed silently, then slowly dropped to his knees. "Listen to me, the three men who just killed Cowlins are getting away. Call your dispatcher—"

"Keep your mouth shut! Facedown on the ground!"

It seemed pointless right then to explain what had happened. Bolan sensed they were a breath away from cutting him down in a hail of lead and buckshot. With no choice but to do what they wanted, he stretched out on the road. The troopers broke from cover to surround him.

**2**

Gary Bannon, a big, tall man wearing a sheepskin coat and black leather gloves, walked out of the darkness of the tree line. He stopped in the outer limits of the glow from the van's headlights. The weathered skin of his hawkish face was drawn tight with tension, and his icy blue eyes drilled into the two men. From inside the van, he could hear the low groans coming from Paul Dugan. Knowing the consequences that could come down on his head from their recklessness, Bannon's anger kept coiling tighter in his belly the longer he stared at the shadowy faces of Bennett and Simmons. Indeed, these three had risked jeopardizing everything he had planned and was about to set into motion. Because of their actions, the Movement could come to a grinding halt. Beneath their stony facades, Bannon could read the fear in their eyes.

"You realize the police could have intercepted your radio transmission?" he said.

Bennett glanced uneasily at Simmons, then turned to Bannon. "It was risky, I know, but we couldn't see any other way. We needed to unload the crate. You wanted the merchandise, right? And there's Dugan, bleeding all over the floor like a stuck pig. He took a slug in the chest. He needs a doctor."

A twig snapped, and Peterson walked out of the shadows. He looked at Bennett and Simmons with contempt.

"That was stupid," he growled, "getting pulled over for speeding by a state trooper with what you had in the van. Not to mention telling us over the radio that you stole the van. Goddamn stupid! How the hell else did you expect it to go down? You three should have known better than to put yourselves in that kind of position."

Bannon spoke up, his voice controlled. "Enough. What's done is done. Go get the Jeep and bring it here," he told Peterson. "We'll bury the crate until it's safe to pick it up again."

When Peterson had left, Bannon said, "Kill these headlights, but turn on the overhead."

As the big man checked the skies for any sign of an aerial search, Bennett went to shut off the van's headlights. Bannon entered the vehicle through its open side door. Beneath the dim overhead light, Dugan looked up at him with eyes full of pain.

Bannon checked the illuminated dial of his Rolex watch. "Say twenty minutes since you left that trooper?" he asked Simmons.

"Give or take a couple of minutes," the man answered.

"Why did you steal the van?"

"On the way back, our truck broke down outside of Durango," Bennett said. "We were out in the middle of nowhere. We came to a ranch. The place was dark, and we figured they wouldn't notice if their van was gone until morning. Look, we had no time, and we had no choice. We'd just picked the crate up."

The big man nodded. "Did the trooper shoot Dugan?"

"No. Another guy I've never seen before came up just as we took down the smoky," Bennett replied.

"A cop?" Bannon asked.

"I don't think so. He was driving a Ford Bronco. The way I read it, he just happened on the scene. He was a big guy, and he moved like a pro," Bennett said, talking fast, looking relieved at having something to tell Bannon. "Dropped Dugan with a hand cannon. It looked like a Magnum."

"Before we got away," Simmons said, "I capped off a few more rounds. The cruiser's tank blew." He paused, then added, "The cops will have a hell of a mess to sort out."

"What about the trooper and the big guy?"

Simmons hesitated, the fear in his eyes again. "I don't know if the trooper's dead, but the last thing I saw was the big guy standing behind the wreckage."

"So, we don't know if the trooper's alive or dead. And we've got a guy with a big gun you've never seen before on the loose who can identify you and the van," Bannon said.

"We don't know that he got a good look at us," Bennett protested.

"Well, you're right about one thing. This is one hell of a mess." Bannon was interrupted by the sound of an engine rumbling through the dark bowels of the woods. The big man turned his attention to the bulky object beneath a tarp, just behind Dugan. The headlights of Peterson's four-wheel-drive Jeep washed over the van, allowing Bannon to see all the blood over the floorboards. It was a mess, all right.

"Bring out the crate," Bannon ordered his men. "Don't drag it through all that blood. Lift it up. The last thing I need is any blood in the Jeep."

The vehicle's lights died as Peterson stopped next to the van. He hopped out, then stepped up into the van beside Bannon, who watched as Bennett and Simmons pulled the tarp off the crate. Dugan moaned pitifully.

"What about me? Help me," Dugan croaked as Bennett and Simmons hefted the large wooden crate from the back of the van. As it passed beneath the overhead light, Bannon saw the words United States Army printed on the crate, and smiled. At least they'd done something right.

"Hang in there, Paul," Bennett said. "We'll get you to a doctor."

"Come on, move it. This whole mountain's going to be crawling with cops," Peterson growled, helping Bennett and Simmons haul the crate out of the van.

Bannon stared down at Dugan as he unbuttoned his sheepskin coat. He listened to his men struggling to put the crate into the back of the Jeep. There was no other way, he knew. Those three had forfeited the right to continue as soldiers in the Movement. It would also send a clear message that Bannon wouldn't tolerate any snafus. He stepped out of the van and saw Bennett and Simmons move away from the back of the Jeep. Slowly he reached inside his coat. As he drew out his .357 Magnum Colt Python, he saw the fear widen their eyes.

"I regret having to do this," he said, leveling the gun on Bennett, "but you understand that the Movement is far more important than the single life of any one of us."

"What do you—?" Bennett cried.

It was the last thing the man said. The Colt cannoned two rounds in lightning succession, blasting two gaping holes in Bennett's chest. The big man triggered another two thundering retorts of instant death. Simmons caught the brutal force of the killing shots at almost point-blank range, two explosions of blood geysering from the exit wounds in his back as he was propelled into the brush.

As the echo of the shots rolled off into the darkness, Bannon walked back to the van. He sighted down the barrel of the Colt Python, drawing a bead on the shock and horror etched on Dugan's face. He then erased the look forever with the last two rounds. He tossed the gun into the woods, then stripped off the shoulder holster and dropped it on the ground. It was a stolen weapon, the serial number filed off. There was probably no way the gun could be traced back to him, but Bannon thought it better not to hold on to it.

Quickly the big man moved past Peterson without looking at him. He checked the Jeep, but found no blood on the vehicle. As he moved up the passenger's side, former FBI Agent Gary Bannon warned Peterson, "Check your shoes for blood before you get in."

BOLAN FIGURED it had been a good twenty minutes since he'd been disarmed, cuffed and tossed into the back of a cruiser. He had told the police what had happened, but clearly they were not yet buying his version.

At the moment the Executioner was a suspect. They'd taken his driver's license and Justice Department ID to run a computer check on him, and rifled through his disabled truck. Before being dumped into the cruiser's back seat, Bolan had given them Hal Brognola's number, a twenty-four-hour emergency line that would put the Colorado law in direct contact with the Man from Wonderland. Bolan suspected they could catch an earful from the big Fed. But right then, Bolan could only wait and watch.

The crime scene was a flurry of activity. Forensics and ballistics personnel were going over the area with a fine-tooth comb. Everything was chalked and roped, and photographed from a complete three-sixty, and every piece of evidence bagged and tagged. Fire extinguishers had been used to put out the flames that had turned Trooper Cowlins's cruiser into a blackened hull. In both directions the highway was blocked off by cruisers. The entire crime scene was lit up by swirling lights, and every few minutes another cruiser seemed to join the investigation. But critical moments had passed since a police chopper had lifted off from the site and vanished somewhere to the north. In the darkness, with thousands of square miles of rugged wilderness, it would be a tall order, Bolan knew, for the law to hunt down the killers anytime soon.

And a cop was dead. The medical examiner had already zipped the plastic bag over Trooper Cowlins before wheeling him into a waiting ambulance.

Impatiently Bolan watched the troopers study maps, talk to each other and use their radios, some of them occasionally glancing at him.

An unmarked car pulled in, and several troopers converged on the vehicle. The door opened and a big man in a leather coat, with a 9-mm pistol on his hip, got out. The Executioner couldn't hear what was being said, but, judging by the nervous looks the troopers were giving Bolan, there was a sudden change in events. One of the troopers handed the man something. Bolan hoped it was his license and Justice Department ID that was getting a hard scouring.

Finally the big man gestured around the crime scene, then headed toward Bolan, another trooper falling in behind him. The door opened and the big man leaned in, his dark eyes betraying a flicker of embarrassment.

"Mr. Belasko, I'm Captain Matt Dawson. I'll be supervising this investigation. Would you please step outside, sir?"

The deep gravelly voice fit the hard granite face. Dawson stepped back, the trooper behind him jiggling a set of keys as if he had a bad case of nerves. Obviously Brognola had straightened out the matter of who "Mike Belasko" was, the identity the Executioner often used as an agent of the U.S. Department of Justice.

Bolan got out and the trooper uncuffed him. It was then, with the adrenaline beginning to subside, that the soldier felt the soreness burning deep into his muscles. He felt a trickle of blood roll down the side of his face, probably caused by flying pieces of shrapnel from the explosion. He flexed his arms, then massaged his numb wrists.

Dawson handed Bolan back his IDs. "You understand how it looked to my men," he said.

Bolan wiped the blood off the side of his face with the back of his hand. He knew that was as close to an apology as he would get.

"That will be all," Dawson told the trooper. "The second you hear anything..."

"Understood, Captain."

Bolan watched Dawson survey the crime scene.

"Trooper Cowlins was a ten-year veteran. He was a personal friend of mine, not to mention a damn fine officer." Dawson sucked in a deep breath. "Damn it. The worst part is he has a wife and three teenaged children."

"You've got three suspects out there, Captain. I'd guess by now they've got a good thirty-minute jump on us."

"I already got the report from my men of your description of the suspects and the vehicle." Dawson scratched a match off his boot heel, then fired up an unfiltered Camel cigarette. He took a deep drag. "I understand you nailed one of the bastards," he said. "From a quick look around, I'd say they must've fired off at least a hundred rounds." He paused. "Even if we'd gotten Cowlins out of here in time and to a hospital, the ME informed me that he'd lost too much blood. The man took four rounds through the chest. Damn those bastards to hell."

Dawson dragged on his cigarette. "Mind if I ask you, Mr. Belasko, what brings a Justice Department agent out to Colorado?"

"R and R."

Dawson grunted. "Yeah. Well, welcome to Colorado. Whatever possessions you have in your vehicle you can take back. The truck looks totaled, but we'll have to impound it as evidence."

"I understand."

"I can help you get another vehicle. But I'd like you to stick around for a few days. There will be a few more questions, maybe something else you'll remember. Not to mention that when we catch these bastards you'll need to ID them."

"I know the drill, Captain," Bolan said. "I don't plan on going anywhere. What about my weapons?"

"If you know the drill, then you know I need to hold on to them. The slug you put into one of those gunmen is evidence."

"I told you I'm not going anywhere. So when you need my Beretta and Desert Eagle, all you have to do is ask. Besides, there's a good chance that the bullet passed through the guy."

"I'll worry about that when the time comes, if and when we recover that .44 slug."

"I've also got a shotgun and a rifle in the truck I'd like back," Bolan added, referring to the Marlin 1894-S lever action in .44 Magnum caliber with scope and the 12-gauge Mossberg 500 shotgun.

"I was told about the riot gun. I didn't know Justice Department agents were issued Magnums."

"Personal choice."

Dawson's gaze narrowed. "That hand cannon of yours is something that could be used to drop a rhino. And we don't get many riots out here where you'd need a military shotgun that could clear out a city block, Mr. Belasko. Something tells me I'm not getting the full picture here.''

"Captain, I'd rather not dance around about my choice of weapons. And everything that happened here went down exactly as I told your men. That's the full picture.

"Besides, it's real simple. I'm a witness. I could just happen to run into those three who killed your trooper, or they could come looking for me. Either way, it would make me feel a lot better to have my weapons.''

Dawson gave a half grin. "Or else you'll call your boss and have him burn my ear about giving you back your guns?''

"I'd rather not. Look, if there's anything I can do to help you catch those men, all you have to do is ask. I'm on your side, all the way. I want them caught just as badly as you do.''

Dawson scanned the mountain range to the north. "We've got over a hundred thousand square miles of some of the wildest real estate in this country. My hunch is they'll ditch the van. In these mountains, with the countless gorges and caves, I figure they'll hide and try to hike it out.'' He seemed to come to a decision. "All right, I'll get you back your weapons before you go. I'll bend procedure a little. You could be right about those men. But until this is over, I want you close."

"Good enough."

Bolan wouldn't come right out and tell Dawson, but the Executioner was in the hunt. He had been there with the trooper, he had taken fire and almost lost his own life. But he suspected something sinister about the trio of gunmen. Something else was going on, and he planned to follow up, do his own investigating. If he got to the killers first, then so be it.

"They've got a badly wounded man on their hands, if he even makes it," Bolan said. "He'll slow them down."

"I don't need to tell you that I want to catch these bastards in the worst way. I don't care how I take them. Dead or alive. I'll make that call when the times comes. And it will come," Dawson assured Bolan.

"They have assault rifles, Captain. M-16s, to be exact. My gut tells me they had something else in that van, and they felt they had to gun down one of your men because of it. Those guys didn't strike me as weekend warriors or dope dealers. They were pros, possibly ex-military or even..."

Bolan let it trail off.

"Even what?"

"Maybe even ex-lawmen."

"You've got all that from just a quick look while under heavy fire from three M-16s and a cruiser blowing up in your face?" Dawson snorted.

"Let's just say I've got a little experience with situations like this."

"What are you saying, Mr. Belasko? We've got some dirty cops out here in the Rockies?"

"No."

"Then what?"

"Are there any paramilitary groups you know of operating in this state?"

The captain dropped his cigarette butt on the ground. "Yeah, we've got them in this state, I'm damned ashamed to say. Aryan Brotherhood, Aryan Nation, the Militiamen, splinter groups of the KKK. Out here, everyone has a weapon. You name it, someone has it, legal or otherwise. The FBI busted a group of right-wing wackos in Denver just a week ago. They were sitting on enough assault rifles, submachine guns and plastic explosives to wipe out half the city." There was a hard pause, then Dawson said, "Mr. Belasko, I'm going to suggest you leave the investigation to me. I appreciate your offer of help, but we'll handle this. Why don't you go get your belongings. I'll have one of my men take you to a motel, and you can get yourself cleaned up. How's your head, by the way?'' he asked as another trickle of blood broke down the Executioner's face.

Bolan wiped the blood away. "Just some scratches."

"Well, get some rest. We'll talk tomorrow."

The Executioner locked stares with Dawson for a moment. Gut instinct warned him that the worst was yet to come.

As he walked to his Bronco, Bolan felt the simmering anger of the troopers all around him. Radios crackled while the lawmen continued to scour the killing ground. In the distance, he spotted the dark shape of the police chopper, its searchlight a glaring finger cutting down into the wooded mountains.

Bolan gave his truck a quick once-over. Steam hissed from the radiator, and a large puddle of oil had collected under the frame. He was about to reach into the truck and retrieve his duffel bags, having decided to leave behind the fishing, hiking and rock-climbing gear and the folded-up canvas tent, when he spotted the latest arrival on the crime scene. He watched the white Jeep Cherokee with swirling barlights on the roof slide to a stop beside the burnt-out cruiser. The driver's door of the Jeep bore the insignia of the Honor County Sheriff. A short but powerfully built man in a sheepskin coat and a white Stetson hat got out of the vehicle and moved into a group of troopers. They engaged in a short talk before Bolan saw the sheriff look his way.

"Here you are, Mr. Belasko," Dawson said, walking up with Bolan's weapons in his hands.

Bolan took his Beretta and Desert Eagle, and donned the holsters. Then he took a sheepskin coat from inside the truck and shrugged it on. He found that the shotgun and rifle had been laid out beside the truck, the weapons obviously having gotten a close inspection by the state police. The trace of a frown danced over Dawson's face as Bolan slipped an arm through the Marlin's strap. The two large duffel bags had already been opened for police eyes, and Bolan tucked the shotgun inside a bag. One bag held a change of clothes and the other was crammed with spare ammo.

Bolan took hold of his bags. "Okay, that should do it."

"What about your gear for your R and R?" Dawson asked.

"I'll decide what to do about it later. Now, how about that motel?"

Bolan followed the captain toward the sheriff and the group of troopers. The sheriff reminded him of a bulldog, with his small, dark eyes and legs like tree trunks.

"Captain," the sheriff said, "I heard what went down. I'd like to help you find those animals."

"That won't be necessary, Sheriff," Dawson replied.

"What do you mean? You'll need every available man on this."

"Belasko," Dawson said, "this is Sheriff Hank Maulin. Sheriff, meet Agent Mike Belasko."

"The Justice guy. Yeah, I heard about you."

The sheriff's tone was openly dismissive. Bolan wondered if the man was going to be a problem.

"Captain," Maulin said, turning back to Dawson, "I'd really like in on this one."

"Sheriff, what I need you to do for me is to take Mr. Belasko and find him some lodging. He'll be staying in Honor County for an indefinite period of time. Whatever he needs, whatever he wants, I expect you to accommodate him.''

Dawson caught the resentful look in the sheriff's eyes. "That won't be a problem for you, will it, Sheriff?''

"No problem, Captain. You know where to find me if you need me.''

"Right. If that's all, Sheriff, you'll have to excuse me. Mr. Belasko, I'll be checking in on you in the morning.''

Dawson walked off. Left alone with the sheriff, Bolan read Maulin's instant dislike of him loud and clear in his stony gaze.

"The door's open,'' Maulin said. He walked over to the driver's side of the Jeep.

Bolan hesitated, giving the crime scene one last look.

"You coming or what?'' Maulin asked. "I don't have all night to wait for you.''

Bolan lingered for another moment, then headed for the vehicle as Maulin got in and banged the door shut.

**3**

Mack Bolan and the sheriff initially rode in silence, heading north along the highway. Maulin, giving Bolan's hardware a suspicious stare, finally broke it.

"So, you're the hero who dropped one of those scumbags, huh?"

"A cop with a family is dead, Sheriff. I'm pretty certain I'm not a hero in their eyes."

Maulin grunted. "What's some Justice Department hotshot doing out here anyway?"

Bolan didn't answer right away, then finally said, "Vacation."

"With all that hardware?" Maulin scoffed. "You've got enough firepower there to make you a one-man SWAT team."

"I like to hunt."

"That a fact? Hunt what?"

"Sheriff, I don't mind telling you that you're starting to bother me."

Maulin lit a cigarette, his hand trembling slightly. He took a deep drag.

"Well, let me tell you something, hotshot," he said, blowing out a thick cloud of smoke in Bolan's direction. "I run a clean county. There's no dope here, there's no criminal activity of any kind and there are no wackos hiding in the mountains. What I'm saying is we don't have any problems like in the big cities in my county. We're decent folk out here."

"What's your point, Sheriff? You don't like or trust strangers passing through who might contaminate your county. Even lawmen."

A smile twisted the sheriff's bulldog face. "You just said it, Mr. Justice. Especially a Fed I don't know, who comes across like he's got all the frigging answers and acts like some avenging angel."

Bolan left his stare on the sheriff for another moment, sizing up the guy. He could understand that Maulin might feel resentful about being relegated to something of a subordinate role to Agent Mike Belasko, but Bolan sensed there was more going on with the sheriff of Honor County than mere resentment. The Executioner smelled a cunning and dangerous animal in Maulin, a man with some degree of power who liked to flex his muscles and who could make life miserable for anyone he didn't care for.

"What about guns, Sheriff?"

"What about them?"

"Dawson implied everyone around here is armed to the teeth."

"That's a man's constitutional right, pal. To bear arms. To protect and defend what's his. This country is going straight to hell, and that dead cop back there is proof enough that all is not well in the good ol' U.S. of A. We've got people running wild in what used to be a great country. I say every decent man has the right to carry a gun anytime, anywhere, and still respect and obey the law. You got any other questions, hero?"

Bolan hadn't expected to get the sheriff's philosophy on the decline of America. But Maulin's intensity strengthened his suspicion that something beyond a straightforward cop killing had happened. But what? Or was he just searching for anything that could prove something more sinister had been played out on the highway? Bolan decided not to pick the sheriff's brain right then. There would be time enough later if he happened to pick up the scent of any paramilitary groups operating in or around Honor County.

"I need transportation, Sheriff, a four-wheel-drive vehicle with plenty of muscle under the hood. If I need four-hundred or so horses put in, I can pay for it."

Maulin blew some more smoke in Bolan's direction. "I don't care what the good captain said. I'm not one to play flunky to any man."

"I'm not asking you to, Sheriff. Can you get me that vehicle or not?"

"I'll see what I can do."

They rode in hard silence for another few miles. Ahead, Bolan spotted a squat, low-lying building off to the side of the road. A neon sign beside the building read Honor Motel. There were a half-dozen trucks, Jeeps or old-model cars in the lot—but no black van. Farther down the road, he saw another building, the lot there also packed with vehicles, as well as men walking in or out of the building or milling around. A bar, Bolan guessed.

Maulin slowed the Jeep, angling for the motel. "You can get a room here."

"Drive past."

"What?" Maulin said.

"I said drive on. What's that place up there?"

"It's a saloon."

"I want to take a quick look at it."

"I don't have time for this," Maulin grumbled.

"Sheriff, I'm asking you to drive up there," Bolan said icily.

Maulin muttered a curse but drove past the motel.

"Pull into the lot," Bolan said.

Scowling, the sheriff swung the vehicle into the lot and parked. A group of four men, weaving slightly from a night of hard drinking, made their way up the stoop. There was a large, smoky plate-glass window that read Saloon of Honor. A few patrons stood drinking on the boardwalk in front of the saloon.

"You allow guys to drink in the open in your county, Sheriff?"

"If I locked up every man for having a drink in this lot, I'd be putting half the county in jail. Are you looking for something in particular, Belasko, or you just trying to piss me off some more?"

Bolan scanned the area, trying to get a feel for anything out of the ordinary. And so apparently was the law, as he spotted the two cruisers parked in the back of the lot. The troopers were also giving every vehicle a hard look, writing down license-plate numbers.

"You think the scumbags who killed Trooper Cowlins would be stupid enough to stop off for a quick beer, maybe brag about what they'd done?" Maulin asked.

"Sometimes the best place to hide is right out in the open. If they're local, maybe they've got buddies. You know, some of those decent citizens you mentioned, who might help them.

"But I've seen enough. You can take me back to the motel."

As Maulin drove back to the motel, Bolan's uneasiness increased. Something didn't feel right. Something nagged at him, telling him that the cop killers were close, perhaps right under his nose.

Maulin braked the Jeep hard in front of the motel office. Bolan gathered up his bags and weapons.

"I want to tell you something, Belasko. I don't give a damn who or what you are, or what you did tonight to get on the captain's good side. But this is *my* county. So if you step out of line, I'll throw you into a cell myself. You read me?"

Bolan opened the door, then threw Maulin a mock salute. "Loud and clear."

"Enjoy your vacation."

The soldier's feet had barely touched the ground when the sheriff floored the engine, kicking up a cloud of dust.

He watched as the vehicle raced off into the night. He didn't intend leaving the county of Honor anytime soon. Not until he'd learned the truth. And he was becoming more certain that there was a dark truth at work, somewhere in the wilderness of the Colorado Rockies.

BOLAN TOOK A ROOM at the very end of the motel, closest to the saloon up the road. Once inside, he locked the door, hit the light and tossed his bags on the bed. He turned on the television, flipping channels until he came to the news. A young female reporter was on the scene of the trooper killing, which was still a beehive of activity. Bolan listened intently.

"What we have learned is that three suspects are still at large. One of them, we were told, was shot by an unidentified man. Whether it was a state policeman who shot the suspect, we don't know at this time."

Okay, Bolan thought, Dawson was trying to keep Mike Belasko out of it. He gave the man silent thanks. The last thing Bolan wanted was to be pegged as the triggerman, especially if he intended to move about freely in Honor. He suspected that Sheriff Maulin would run his mouth, just to cause "the Justice hotshot" a little notoriety that would encumber his movements and make the locals uneasy in his presence.

Bolan listened to the newscast for another few moments: manhunt underway; roadblocks all over the state; a description of the van, but sketchy IDs on the suspects. It was nothing that he didn't already know. He turned down the volume and dialed Hal Brognola at Stony Man Farm.

"Yeah, it's me," Bolan said when the big Fed came on the other end.

"You take a little R and R and all hell breaks loose," Brognola said in a grim voice touched with concern. "I heard about the trooper. I'm sorry. It's always tough when we lose one of our own."

"I appreciate your setting things straight with the state police."

"What happened?"

Bolan gave it to Brognola, quick and short.

"So, you've got to hang around until they catch these guys."

"Looks that way."

"Hold on a second. I know that tone of voice. Something tells me you're not going to wait on the sidelines."

"I'm staying in Honor County." Bolan gave Brognola his motel room and phone number. "And you're right. I'm putting myself in this. I've got a feeling there's some trouble out here."

"What kind of trouble?"

"These guys who killed the trooper were armed with M-16s. I need you to do a little digging. What I want is all intel on any paramilitary right-wing groups, hate groups, that are operating, or are even suspected of operating, in this state. I need the names and last locations of any members of groups you can come up with. There was a bust of some right-wing fanatics in Denver last week. You might want to start there. I also want you to run a background check on the local sheriff, Hank Maulin."

"What's the problem with the local law? You think this Maulin might be dirty?"

"I think he's going to be a problem. I'll know more once you get back to me. It's just a hunch, but I'm picking up some signals I don't like."

"Okay, I'll get right on it. What are you going to do in the meantime?"

"Go and have a beer," Bolan replied.

MATT DAWSON STEPPED into the light that burned overhead from the hovering chopper. Right away, seeing his men standing over the three bodies or searching the van, he knew they'd found their cop killers.

"What have we got?" Dawson asked a trooper who was holding a big gun by means of a pencil through the trigger guard.

"It's a .357 Magnum, Captain. Looks like whoever did this emptied the whole magazine into them. Two rounds apiece, seems like. The serial number's been filed off the gun, stolen, I'm sure. The holster was dropped by the van."

Dawson cursed. He felt cheated, and now he had a mystery on his hands, a new killer or killers out there who had done this.

"How about those assault rifles?" Dawson asked.

"In the van. Three M-16s, and a box loaded with a few dozen clips. These guys were ready to start a war."

No kidding, Dawson thought, going to check the body in the van. The triggerman had blown off the guy's face at point-blank range, leaving behind nothing but gobs of brains and blood decorating the walls of the van.

Dawson moved on to the other two bodies, staring down at their unseeing eyes. The chopper's searchlight washed over the dead faces for just a moment, and he felt his stomach tighten and the hairs rise on his nape.

"Somebody give me a flashlight." Dawson took the flashlight from a trooper and shone it on the face of one of the victims. "I'll be damned," he muttered.

"What is it, Captain?"

"I know this man. His name's Steve Bennett. He used to work for the Denver PD."

**4**

The Saloon of Honor was pretty much what Bolan had expected—a lot of guys in cowboy hats and boots, some of them with buck knives or what looked like commando daggers sheathed on their hips, a lot of boozing, and a thick cloud of cigar and cigarette smoke hanging in the air. A group of guys played darts in the far corner of the room, while the two pool tables were surrounded by a few patrons who were tossing bills onto the green felt. Lassos, as well as mounted elk, deer and bearheads, decorated the walls. Four waitresses, wearing short frilly skirts and cowgirl boots, served the customers. A jukebox wailed a country-and-western song.

Bolan made his way to the bar, where he found an empty stool. He noticed some of the customers sizing him up. He wondered how many men, like himself with the Desert Eagle in a shoulder holster beneath his coat, were carrying concealed side arms. But the Executioner was there for only a simple civilian recon.

He scanned the crowd, memorizing faces, but primarily looking for three cop killers, at the most, or at the least, overhearing something that would nail down his suspicions that there were some paramilitary fanatics among the locals. More and more, he felt he was onto a trail of trouble. There were men in the bar who seemed the kind who wouldn't hesitate to bust up, maim or even kill a man. Even the occasional bursts of raucous laughter held a grim note, telling Bolan that with one wrong word or look, fists would be flying or knives flashing. He began to think that Sheriff Maulin's town wasn't nearly as honorable as its namesake.

Bolan avoided making extended eye contact, aware that he was very much a stranger in town. The last thing he needed was to be involved in a fight and deal with the law again.

A bleached-blond cowgirl with a lot of makeup smiled at Bolan, but his gaze moved on, coming to rest on four men sitting at a large round table in the back of the room. One of them, a guy with a sharp hawkish face, was staring at Bolan from under hooded eyes. Hawk-face sat with his back to the wall, while his cronies sipped their beers and smoked in silence. The Executioner's sixth sense came to life as he watched Hawkface take his measure.

"What are you drinking, pal?"

Bolan slowly broke Hawkface's stare and turned to the bartender, a man so huge he could have been carved right out of the Rockies.

"A beer."

"We only got American beer."

"Sounds good."

The mountain-sized bartender went to get his drink.

Suddenly a voice broke through the general hum of conversation. "Hey! You're starting to piss me off, Little Joe."

Bolan saw the two pool players reflected in the mirror behind the bar. One of them was a big man with curly red hair, a large hunting knife on his hip. Red was scowling at the other player, a man with shoulder-length raven black hair, dark skin and sharp cheekbones. "Little" Joe stood about six-five and weighed approximately two-twenty, Bolan estimated, with big shoulders and a muscled chest beneath his wildly colored serape. Under Red's glaring eye, Little Joe scooped up a fistful of cash from the table. Bolan kept watching in the mirror, as the laughter and talk died in the bar. Little Joe, sporting a triumphant grin, pocketed the cash and killed a shot of whiskey before working on a mug of beer.

"Again?" Little Joe asked, still grinning as he cued up his stick.

"Damn right," Red growled. "Rack 'em. Double or nothing."

"I thought the loser racks?"

"I'll be damned before I let someone take my money, then try and order me around. Rack 'em yourself."

Little Joe shrugged. His smile vanished, but he racked the balls. The hostile looks Little Joe was receiving from the other patrons told Bolan the big Native American was on his own.

"That'll be two bucks," the bartender told Bolan, setting his bottle of beer on the counter.

Bolan dug into his pocket. Out of the corner of his eye, he noticed Hawkface was still watching him.

IT HAD TO BE HIM—the big guy with the big gun—that Bennett had described. Gary Bannon knew the look, the walk, the aura of a man who knew the face of death from personal experience, who had walked away from countless kill-or-be-killed situations a winner. This stranger was trouble,

Bannon decided. The guy hadn't just strolled in for a quick couple of beers.

"What's the problem?" Bannon heard Peterson ask him.

"The big guy sitting at the bar by himself who just came in," Bannon said. "Don't make it obvious, but that's our hero."

One by one, Peterson, Wilkins and Thomas let their eyes rove around the room before finding the big stranger.

They returned to their drinks.

"You think he's a cop?" Wilkins asked.

"He doesn't look like any cop to me," Peterson countered.

"He isn't any cop," Bannon said.

"If he's the shooter, then the police wouldn't have let him go unless he was one of them," Thomas pointed out.

"I don't know *what* he is, but that's our boy," Bannon said. "See the bulge beneath his coat? If the guy's not packing a cannon, I'll buy the beer for the next week."

"So, what the hell are we supposed to do now?" Thomas wanted to know. "Why are we even still here?"

"To catch the latest word. You saw all the smokys out in the lot earlier," Bannon replied.

"In a small town like this, news will spread real fast if they come up with anything solid. Just relax. Everything at the compound has been taken apart and taken down. There's not a trace of anything that will make anyone the least bit suspicious. Everything is underground."

"But that doesn't mean it's safe. There are some big mouths in this town," Peterson said.

Bannon knew the man had a point. Sure, their compound had been disassembled, all weapons, radio and surveillance equipment put underground near their base, but that didn't mean the state police wouldn't find the place and tear it apart. And when they found the bodies of Bennett, Dugan and Simmons the cops could easily conclude that the executions were the work of some locals.

"So, do we lay low and ride it out?" Wilkins asked.

"No," Bannon said. "We can work around their investigation. As long as everyone keeps their mouths shut, we'll be fine. You guys know the routine. Shouldn't be too hard to get this thing to blow over and have them looking in other directions. And about those big mouths. I hear about the first man, inside or outside our circle, who gets some cop suspicious, that man will answer to me.''

''If you don't wipe that stupid grin off your face, I'll wipe it off for you, Little Joe,'' Bannon heard Johnny Smith shout.

Along with his men, Bannon watched the scene at the pool table. Bannon knew Smith was one of the local would-be toughs, but without his buddies around him, he was pretty much a coward and a bully. It was the biggest reason Bannon didn't want him in the movement, even though Smith had practically begged him to join. Bannon only had time for the real thing, not wannabes who would probably turn tail and run for their lives the first time the odds weren't stacked in their favor.

Bannon waited for the game's outcome. For almost an hour, the big Native American had been beating Smith in eight ball. Bannon figured Little Joe had won at least three hundred dollars. With a double or nothing game on the line, and with Smith fueled by plenty of whiskey and his buddies looking on, trouble was only a few minutes away. There was no doubt in Bannon's mind as to who would win the pool game. It was what would happen after that would prove interesting.

Bannon watched, his gaze narrowing. The double or nothing game had come down to two shots. Little Joe had a long shot on the eight ball, which was right up against the far cushion, meaning he'd have to bank it back at him. If he missed, although he'd been making tougher shots than that all night, Smith had his only ball, the three, two inches right in front of the side pocket. Smith was nervously licking his lips. Someone snapped off the jukebox, and the whole room went quiet as Little Joe threw back his serape and cued his stick.

"Where you think you're putting that eight, Indian?" Smith asked.

Little Joe tapped the side pocket beside him. "Back at me."

Smith chuckled, but it was a laugh that lacked confidence. "If you miss, the game's over."

"If the Indian makes that shot," Peterson said, "I've got a feeling he's going to get stomped."

Bannon let his gaze flicker to the bar, where the big guy sat facing the mirror.

"I don't think that's going to happen," Bannon said. He sipped his beer. "Why don't we enjoy the show?"

Mack Bolan silently pulled for Little Joe to drop the shot. Guys like Red were only brave when they had the advantage of size, weapons, or, as at the moment, numbers. The Executioner read the look of senseless anger in the faces of Red's cronies. It was all ready to blow up, but Bolan didn't intend to sit by and watch. Little Joe didn't know it yet, but he wasn't alone.

Little Joe moved to the far end of the table where he squatted, measuring the angle of the shot. Red cursed him impatiently. Grinning, Little Joe got up and finished his beer, clearly enjoying the moment, then sauntered to the other end of the table. The guy had nerve, Bolan gave him that.

The man took his time cueing up before tossing the serape back over his shoulder. His expression now set hard, Little Joe bent as he lined up the shot. He stroked the cue ball, which traveled down the table. It banged the eight ball high and just to the side, sending it rolling hard and fast back at Little Joe. It was over in the next heartbeat as the ball dropped into the hole.

"I believe you owe me six hundred dollars," he announced into the silence.

Red nodded, dug into his pocket and flipped a wad of bills onto the railing.

"Go ahead, pick it up. You won it, didn't you?"

Little Joe hesitated, then as he reached for the money, Red did exactly what Bolan had been expecting. He cracked a right off Little Joe's jaw and dropped him on his back.

"The day you kick my ass, man to man," Red said to the fallen man, "is the day you can take my money."

Someone in the crowd laughed.

Bolan got off his stool. Red kicked Little Joe in the ribs before the Executioner came around the corner of the table.

"That'll be enough," Bolan said.

"Who the hell are you?" Red snarled.

Bolan looked around at the citizens of Honor. They seemed to stare back at him, hungrily anticipating the spill of blood. Little Joe groaned and struggled to sit up against the side of the table.

The soldier addressed Red, looking him dead in the eye. "I'm the guy who can make you regret the day you were born if you don't pay this man his money. Then you will apologize to him and buy him a drink."

Red looked at his buddies. "Who is this asshole? Anybody here know this joker?" He laughed.

Bolan took a step toward Little Joe and started to bend as if to help him stand. The roundhouse was telegraphed all the way, and the soldier was ready for it. He ducked the fist then hammered a right deep into Red's gut. The air belched from Red's mouth and his eyes bulged. Bolan delivered a lightning left hook that cracked off the guy's jaw and sent him reeling across the table. He then pivoted to take on any newcomers, but no one moved on him. In the next moment, he found out why as Red yelled a curse, snaring Bolan's attention.

Red had pulled his knife. It had an ivory handle, and the blade, at least eight inches long, was honed to a razor sharpness. One of the waitresses screamed for somebody to do something, but no one did a thing except watch. Bolan held his ground as Red moved toward him. His eyes wild, the man brought the blade down in a sweeping arc meant to slice Bolan's face in half. The soldier waited until the critical last instant, then jumped back, the blade sweeping down and past him, the slipstream of steel brushing his face. Adrenaline bursting through him, Bolan grabbed Red's knife hand, using the man's momentum to give the blade a savage thrust down and in.

Red's scream was piercing and bone chilling as the knife was driven almost to the hilt into his thigh.

"Behind you!" Little Joe yelled.

Wheeling, Bolan caught a glimpse of the pool cue aimed at the back of his head. The Executioner ducked, then heard the sickening crack of bone as the cue smashed into Red's face. Not missing a beat, Bolan exploded a straight right into the face of the guy who'd tried to take his head off with the pool stick. He connected with the guy's nose, taking out some teeth in the process and sending him spilling to the pool table under a gummy spray of blood and flying teeth. The soldier saw Little Joe leap to his feet and bulldoze into another citizen of Honor with his shoulder.

Another of Red's buddies charged Bolan, but the Executioner all but shattered the guy's jaw with a sweeping hook kick. As the guy backpedaled for the wall, Bolan followed up with three lightning lefts and a final right cross, sending him crashing into the wall.

Suddenly three gunshots rang out, and Matt Dawson's voice bellowed over the mayhem. "The next man who moves will spend more than a night in jail."

Bolan waited as Dawson surveyed the area, finally telling one of the troopers accompanying him to inspect the injured men.

The trooper checked each one for a pulse, then nodded at Dawson. "They'll live."

Dawson addressed the men of Honor. "I suggest you get your buddies here to a hospital. You—" he said to Bolan "—outside."

"Damn right, arresting him," the bartender said.

"For what? Cleaning up the garbage?" Dawson barked.

The bartender scowled, looking set to protest.

"You say another word," Dawson warned, "and I'll shut you down now."

The captain waited for Bolan to move. The soldier knew he was pushing his luck, but he picked up the money and handed it to Little Joe. The big man took it without saying a word, but Bolan could read the gratitude in his eyes.

Outside, Bolan turned to face Dawson, who was clearly fighting to control his anger.

"It doesn't take you long to get acquainted with the locals, does it, Mr. Belasko? What the hell was that all about?"

"Would you believe I was just doing my civic duty?"

"Don't get smart with me," Dawson said shortly.

"I was being honest. You were the one who said something about cleaning up the garbage."

"I can pretty much imagine what happened in there. I can also tell you're packing that cannon. If you'd pulled that thing in there, I'd be busting you right now, self-defense or not. But I didn't come here to clean up your mess. We found our three cop killers. I need you to identify them. Identify the bodies, that is."

Bolan stared at him. "That was quick."

"It was too quick. Somebody other than the police got to them first."

"What do you mean?"

"Somebody shot the three of them dead at point-blank range. And we've got to find out who, and why."

**5**

Mack Bolan followed Dawson to the crime scene deep in the woods, a good mile off the main highway. The troopers went about their homicide detail, with the area lit up like day by flashlights, cruisers and a hovering chopper.

Dawson led Bolan to the first two bodies. They were uncovered, lying in pools of blood near the edge of some brush. The expression of shock and horror on the face of one of the corpses gave Bolan the distinct impression that these men had known their killer.

Although he had been under heavy fire, Bolan had gotten a good enough look at the gunmen's faces to know they had been the ones who had murdered Trooper Cowlins.

"It's them," Bolan told Dawson. He looked toward the troopers taking pictures of the van, the camera flashes popping over the body he could see inside.

"That's the third one," Dawson said. "His face was blown off, but there's a hole in his chest big enough to put my fist in. That would be the one you dropped."

Bolan sensed the man was disturbed about something. "Did you know them?"

Dawson hesitated for a second, then answered, "One of them or rather of him." He jerked a nod at one of the bodies on the ground. "He was a former Denver police officer."

Bolan felt a chill race down his spine. Cops killing cops?

Dawson nodded. "Yeah, there you have it. An ex-lawman gunning down a state trooper. Where the hell's the sheriff?" he barked at his men.

"He's on the way, Captain," a trooper called back.

"The one you recognized, was he local?" Bolan asked.

"Yes. He'd lived here for three years, according to the computer printout. No criminal record. He was divorced, had a couple of kids up north. The man lived a quiet life here in Honor, quite a model citizen."

"Maybe too quiet," Bolan muttered. "My guess would be the other two were also local."

"That's why I want Maulin here. Hopefully the good sheriff can at least identify the other one who still has a face."

"What about his police service record?" Bolan asked.

"If you mean was he a good cop, he had an outstanding record as a police officer. Fact is, the man retired with one of the best service records that department has seen. Felony arrests, community service, you name it."

"What was his name?" Bolan would be able to pass it on to Brognola later.

"Steve Bennett. Look, Belasko," Dawson went on, "this will be an ongoing investigation. I've got a dead trooper and now a triple homicide, and I don't need to tell you they're probably tied in. If you're thinking about striking out and doing your own detective work, forget it. Don't step on my toes. After that little scene back there at the bar, I could make life real tough for you. Do you understand what I'm saying?"

"I already told you what happened."

"Yes, you did, and I know it went down exactly the way you told it, which is the only reason I'm cutting you any slack. But all you did was make things a whole lot harder on yourself. Those men have friends. This is a tight community, and like most small towns, strangers aren't easily trusted. By kicking the hell out of some stupid locals, you just made a lot of enemies.''

Dawson moved off. Bolan took in the crime scene, his mind filled with the recent events. It didn't make sense. A former cop with a sterling record was involved in the murder of a state trooper, then he was murdered, along with the other killers, by an unknown party. They had been hiding something, or someone, Bolan was sure of it. Narcotics? Weapons? Or were they links in a chain of some conspiracy in the process of unfolding, disposable liabilities who'd put someone or something in danger of being exposed when they'd killed Trooper Cowlins? Whatever, there was no doubt in Bolan's mind that whomever executed these men knew them. Hawkface flashed through the soldier's mind. There was something about the guy and his cronies, the way Hawkface had sized him up in the bar.

Bolan snapped out of his grim reflections as he saw the sheriff's white Jeep Cherokee pull up just outside the crime scene. Maulin got out and banged the door shut. He hadn't traveled alone.

Bolan met Little Joe's eyes. The way the man was sitting in the Jeep, with his hands behind his back, told the soldier Little Joe was cuffed.

He tensed for a confrontation as Maulin stormed up to Dawson, the sheriff glaring murder at Bolan before addressing the captain. "I'm placing Belasko here under arrest."

Dawson glanced at Bolan as if to tell him he'd handle it. "For what?"

"Assault. The same charge I've got on the Indian, among a couple of others."

"Forget it, Sheriff," Dawson said brusquely.

"Forget it, hell! I just saw three men wheeled off to hospital. They've got enough broken bones in their faces to lay them up for weeks and have them eating through tubes. I've got a man with a knife in his leg who'll probably have a limp the rest of his life. If that doesn't qualify as assault, then I don't know what the hell does."

Dawson put some steel into his eyes and voice. "Sheriff, I was there. I read the situation for what it was, right off. And I got the story from Mr. Belasko, who, you seem to be forgetting, is a federal agent. And in case you don't know, his authority carries more weight than both of our badges put together. So, you can take all the statements you want, but his version is the version I believe. As for that guy with the knife in his leg, he damn sure had it coming to him. Fact is, he's lucky Belasko didn't decide to put that blade through his heart. So back off. And I suggest you cooperate with myself and Agent Belasko here."

Maulin's face hardened with resentment. "What are you saying? Some stranger, and I don't give a damn if he's a Fed or not, can just come into my town and start committing assault?"

"He, and that man you've got in your Jeep, Sheriff," Dawson responded, "were the ones who were assaulted first. Three of your local tough guys bit off more than they could chew, got their butts whipped and that's that. Don't waste my time with this petty stuff. I've got a dead trooper and three dead killers right here. Lay off Belasko, he's with me. Now, I need an identification from you on one of these corpses."

"What about Little Joe?" Bolan asked Dawson.

The captain suddenly appeared weary of running interference for the Executioner. "He'll be released before we go."

Before Maulin could protest, Dawson led him to the bodies.

Bolan watched the sheriff closely as he studied the two men. The Executioner thought he detected something that looked like fear on the man's face.

"That's Steve Bennett."

"And the other one? Do you recognize him?" Dawson prodded.

"His name is Doug Simmons."

"Both residents of your county, right?" Dawson said.

"What's going on here, Captain?" Maulin asked.

"I'm telling you these are my cop killers," Dawson growled.

"Are you sure? I knew these men," Maulin protested. "They never did an illegal thing the whole time they lived here. They were...."

"They were what, Sheriff?" Dawson pushed. "I know one was a former Denver police officer. Maybe you can tell me what this Simmons did."

"I heard he used to work for the Secret Service."

Ten-to-one, Bolan thought, the third dead cop killer was also a former lawman of some sort.

Dawson muttered a curse. Yeah, Bolan thought, the mystery became even more tainted with that insidious element.

Long moments of hard silence passed before Dawson said, "Sheriff, starting tomorrow morning, every citizen in your town will be questioned. I want a complete list of everyone who lives in or around Honor County, complete with any files of any arrests you've made in the past three years. Anyone who doesn't show, I'll go looking for them. Anyone suddenly skips town, I don't give a damn if they claim they've gone to Miami to bury their blue-haired grandmother, I'll camp out in your county until they are brought to me."

"Come on, Captain," Maulin implored, "you think someone in my county had anything to do with this?"

"That's exactly what I think, Sheriff."

Maulin let his gaze fall on the dead men. "How... I don't understand. They were good men. I knew them personally."

Bolan decided it was time to shake some trees. "Well, these good men, Sheriff, killed a law-enforcement officer and almost killed me. Something tells me you need to look a little harder at the fine citizens of your town."

As Maulin's expression turned stony with anger, Bolan told Dawson, "I want Little Joe released to me, and all charges against him dropped."

"Sheriff," Dawson said, "you heard the man. Let the man go. I don't have all night to referee whatever the hell's going on between you and Agent Belasko."

Maulin looked ready to protest, but Bolan cut the sheriff off, adding, "And he had six hundred dollars on him. Make sure he gets it back."

"You implying I would steal the Indian's money?" Maulin asked.

Bolan ignored him. "Captain, I need a vehicle."

"Damn it, Belasko," Dawson said wearily, "how many favors do you need from me in one night?"

"Just some wheels."

"Get him a vehicle, tonight," Dawson told Maulin.

"You got enough money, Belasko?" the sheriff asked.

"Maulin, you're trying my patience," Dawson snapped. "Get him a vehicle. Belasko, I'll be by in the morning to talk to you. Now, if you don't mind, I've got a homicide investigation here. Both of you, get the hell out of my face.''

BOLAN GOT HIS WHEELS, a black Chevy Blazer with a four-fifty-four engine. Sheriff Maulin knew right where to go. An old-timer on the outskirts of the county had been roused from a deep slumber, but when he'd seen the wad of money in Bolan's hand, he had quickly come alive. With a yard clogged with all manner of vehicles, Bolan didn't have much trouble finding what he wanted. The Chevy Blazer looked and sounded reliable after he had given it a test drive and a quick inspection under the hood. From there, Bolan had parted company with Maulin, after getting Little Joe released to him and after the sheriff had returned the big man's money.

Bolan could feel Little Joe's curious stare as they headed north. So far, they had passed only one roadblock. Bolan had flashed his Justice ID, but the troopers had already seemed to know who he was, and they'd let him pass.

"I appreciate what you did for me tonight, Mr. Belasko," Little Joe said. "If I can return the favor, all you need to do is ask."

"Okay. You can do it right now. Tell me about this town. More specifically tell me what, if anything, you know about any paramilitary or hate groups in this area."

"They're here," was all the man said.

Just like that, Bolan had his answer.

"You make it sound like it's something as American as baseball and apple pie."

"I hear you're a federal agent," Little Joe went on. "So it shouldn't surprise you that these groups exist wherever there are people who have guns and the will to use them. It's all about power and who has it, or who has lost it and wants it back. Or those who have never had it and don't care if they live or die because, according to them, death is preferable to life."

"Do you hate this town?" Bolan asked after a moment of thoughtful silence.

"Hate's a pretty strong word. I would say I tolerate it."

"Why do you stay then?"

"I was born here, and I've lived here all of my life," Little Joe replied.

"Have you had any trouble like tonight before?" Bolan asked.

"Do you mean have I seen the inside of the good sheriff's jail cell? Yes, I've been there a number of times. I'm grateful you had my money returned to me. It's not the first time

Maulin's kept my winnings after he's tossed me in for a night to sleep off a bellyful of firewater and cool down my, to use his words, 'smartass Injun mouth.' The fact that I didn't question why he never gave my money back is probably the only reason I've never been in his jail for more than a night, or had any more serious charges other than drunk and disorderly thrown at me."

Bolan was beginning to form a bad opinion about Maulin and the town of Honor. "Mind if I ask how you would have gotten home?"

"My daughter, Rebecca. She'll sometimes come and pick me up if I've had too much whiskey. Or I walk home. I avoid driving if I drink. That would be practically begging the good sheriff to take my hard-earned money." Little Joe cut his wry grin. "Besides, it's against the law."

"It's a long walk from the saloon."

"I like the exercise. I can breathe the clean mountain air, get in touch with my Cherokee roots. Maybe do a little war dance to bring my ancestors to life so they can guide me through this world." Little Joe smiled sardonically. "Why don't we get back to what you really want to know?"

Bolan returned the grin with one of his own. "Okay. The names of anyone you know who's involved in any paramilitary group in this county or its perimeter."

"All of them are."

"That include Maulin?"

"All of them are," the man repeated.

Bolan saw he wasn't about to get much more information out of Little Joe as the man turned to stare out of the window.

"You've told me enough," Bolan said.

"For now?"

"Yes."

Little Joe lifted an eyebrow. "So, I still owe you."

"You don't owe me a thing. What I did for you tonight I would've done for any man."

They rode in silence for another few miles, until Little Joe pointed to a trail up ahead. "You can stop there. My home is only a little way up the trail."

Bolan stopped. Little Joe got out, then stood in the car's doorway, looking back at Bolan.

"They are not all bad people in this town," he said. "But there are enough of them to either contaminate the few good ones left, or frighten them into keeping silent. Tell you what, Mr. Belasko, why don't you meet me at the coffee shop in the morning. Make it ten o'clock. I'll buy. There's someone I think you should meet.''

''I'll be there.''

Little Joe nodded and moved off, disappearing into the darkness of the trail. Bolan turned the Blazer around. He had a lot of ground to cover with Brognola when he got back to the motel.

Instinct warned the Executioner that the morning was going to bring new trouble.

BUT IT WAS the night that once again brought the potential of more trouble.

As he neared the motel, Bolan saw them in the headlights of his Blazer. Hawkface and his cronies lounged about their Jeep, arms folded, waiting in front of the door to Bolan's room. Whether they were armed or what exactly they wanted, Bolan didn't know. But he was quite sure it wasn't a social call meant to welcome him to town.

He slid the Blazer into the space beside the Jeep, killed the engine and slowly got out.

## 6

The Executioner walked to the front of the Blazer, his gaze locked on Hawkface. There he stopped, waiting on them. All it took was an up-close hard look at the men for Bolan to know they weren't homegrown locals. He sensed a rage, a hate and a fear in them that was as dangerous as anything he had encountered anywhere in the killing fields. Instinct told Bolan that he was in the presence of four paramilitary fanatics. Even stronger was his hunch that Hawkface had killed the three men back in the woods. But he needed more than instinct.

Finally Bolan broke the silence. "Is this where you tell me to get out of town by sunup?"

Hawkface looked around at his cronies, then laughed. It was a deep, mocking sound. "Actually no. I just wanted to meet the hero who'd tried to save that trooper. Don't be surprised that I know. Both good and bad news travels fast in a small town. Pays for a man to have friends, too."

Bolan knew. Hawkface was issuing him a warning.

"Saw you in the bar," Hawkface went on. "Some real pretty work. Of course, you didn't exactly endear yourself to some of the locals. But you move real nice, like a man who has a purpose and a whole lot of experience. I mean, even if you were gone from here tomorrow, I think you've left your mark."

"Well, if you're finished congratulating me," Bolan said, "I'll say good-night."

"No," Hawkface said, his voice taking on a threatening tone, "that isn't all. Maybe I can save you some digging. My name is Gary Bannon. I'm a former FBI agent. I used to be special agent in charge of the field office in Houston."

Bolan decided to play Bannon's game, knowing it was leading somewhere. "Why are you telling me this?"

"Like I said, to save you the bother. Everything about myself, Wilkins, Thomas and Peterson here, it's all out in the open, a matter of public record."

A grim smile cut Bolan's lips. "You're saying you've got nothing to hide?"

"You got it, Mr. Belasko."

Bolan tried to hide his surprise but his expression allowed Bannon a triumphant chuckle. Either the press had discovered and leaked his identity, or someone had a big mouth and an even bigger reason to tell Bannon about Justice Department Agent Mike Belasko. Sheriff Hank Maulin, perhaps.

"I used to believe in this great country, long ago when I was with the FBI," Bannon said. "One day, something just hit me. I saw everything going to hell, all the way from the top where the so-called lawmakers and the lawmen were helping themselves to a bigger piece of the pie than they were entitled to, right down to your basic guy on the streets, punks who were armed with more firepower than most big-city police departments. And the courts just slapped them on the wrist because some lawyer got the courts and media to portray these punks as misunderstood and disadvantaged. I got fed up with all those so-called special interest groups whining not for equal rights under the law, but special rights. You know why they do that?" Bannon paused for breath. "Because too many of them are either inferior, or feel inferior and know they can't cut it on their own merits. Meanwhile our own government buys into that disadvantaged crap. There's not a politician in Washington who has the stones to call it like it is and take care of business. We have to change all that and put the power back where it belongs.''

"Was that a recruitment speech?" was all Bolan said.

"It's a message to you about our times, friend. It's a message to you that things will be made right again. It's a message that the Right Hand of God is going to come down and rid this country of all undesirables.''

"You'll excuse me if I disagree with all your messages.''

"What you think is unimportant to me.'' Bannon's expression took on an almost demonic slant, but he kept it leashed. "I know firsthand that the system protects the very animals I risked my life to put away. Let me tell you a story. One day, this bunch of wetbacks comes across the border in New Mexico. They go on a bank robbing and murdering spree, then cross over into Texas. We've got a half-dozen banks taken down, carjacking, house breaking, rape, murder, all by a bunch of psychopaths who re-sent the gringos to the north who have everything they want. So FBI Special Agent Gary Bannon forms a special task force to go after these murdering wetbacks. What happens? Special Agent Bannon corners them in a barrio. He's outmanned and outgunned, but he storms their safehouse and kills every last one of them. Saves the courts a whole lot of trouble. Probably saves a whole lot of innocent lives, too. Only the FBI says the shootings were suspicious, that my self-defense killings of those murderers were executions. Only my version is the only eyewitness version. So, to keep the public outcry over these special interest groups to an embarrassing minimum, I'm forced into early retirement. Or I'm pretty much threatened with being 'dismissed with prejudice.' Sort of a dishonorable discharge. Meaning I could never work for the U.S. government I risked my life to defend and protect, much less ever hope to work as a law-enforcement officer again."

Bolan realized the guy was far more dangerous than he'd first suspected.

"Sounds like the FBI made the right decision," Bolan said, tight-lipped. "Canning you, that is."

Bannon stiffened and Bolan tensed himself for an explosion. The ex-FBI agent took a step forward. He bared his teeth, showing Bolan a cold smile. "You just told me everything I need to know about you," he said. "Have a nice night."

Bolan held his ground as Bannon got into the Jeep, followed by his cronies.

The soldier knew, more than ever, that he had to stay in Honor and fight it out. Already, the real law had proved itself no match for rabid fanatics, fueled by hate and a twisted idealism, and armed with the heavier firepower. But what Gary Bannon had neglected to say was that he had just told the Executioner everything *he* needed to know.

The Jeep's engine was revved and the vehicle sluiced in reverse across the lot before racing off down the highway. Moments later, it had vanished into the night.

"DO YOU THINK that was smart?" asked Peterson, as he guided the Jeep toward their secondary safehouse.

"It was necessary," Bannon answered. "I needed to know who and what we're dealing with. Plus the guy took down one of our people, which forced me to do something I would rather not have done. Kill our own."

Wilkins sounded anxious as he said, "He isn't a cop. What if he tries to stop us? He's got the look of someone who can handle things. We've already seen him in action."

Bannon couldn't agree more, but he knew he had to keep his troops under control, pumped up and focused on their main objective. "This Mike Belasko is only one man, remember that. I read him as a guy who won't go to the police, but who will try and handle things himself. What you saw back there is a lone wolf."

"But one who is onto the scent of blood," Thomas put in, a little too nervously for Bannon's liking.

"We stay on course," Bannon growled. "Call everyone and set up a meet for tomorrow, early afternoon. No weapons, no literature. I don't even want to see a knife on anyone. We'll use the emergency lodge."

Peterson shot Bannon a sharp look. "Kind of risky, don't you think? Calling a session with all the heat around here now."

"No more risky than what we've got set to go down in Washington." Bannon clenched his jaw. "There is too much at stake for us to hide in a hole and wait for the state police to pull out. And they will pull out if everyone keeps their mouths shut.''

"There are a few I'm worried about maybe squawking to the police," Thomas said.

Bannon decided it was time to let them know how much he wanted this kicked into overdrive. "Listen to me. We didn't spend the past three years running guns to inner city gangs, putting this operation together and setting up overseas connections to bail out now. I'll tell you this much, and you know I am damn deadly serious. Any problems from the law, any fingers point our way and we will burn that town to the ground before we leave. And we have the firepower, the expertise and the guts to pull it off." Bannon stared at them. "Anyone wants out, let me know now."

Each man assured Bannon they were in. Damn right, they would stay on. What was going to happen in Washington was only the beginning. From there, they could hire out their services and begin to collect some real fat paydays. It would be open season on all the scum and undesirables of the world. Already the man they knew only as the Syrian had a few jobs lined up for the Right Hand of God, so they were set to go on a tour of death, violence and sabotage. All the Syrian needed was proof that they were serious, and those Swiss bank accounts could start swelling.

"The second shipment is already on the way," Bannon told them. "We'll have enough firepower at our disposal to take on any lone wolves and any kind of law. Our reinforcements are set to go. A couple of hours ago I spoke with our people in Kansas—they're champing at the bit. Our escape route is guaranteed, and we've got the fastest Lear jets ready to fly us out of the country. It's a lock."

Bannon let the information sink in. He noticed that Wilkins avoided making eye contact with him. If the man was having trouble finding his nerve, was thinking about going to the police, then Bannon would have to find out quickly. Wilkins was ex-Army, one of the few of the group who weren't ex-law. It had been Wilkins's connections that had landed the Right Hand of God much of its heavier firepower. He knew a lot about the inner workings of the movement, knew the game plan set to go down in D.C. Wilkins knew too much.

Bannon stared at the wooded countryside flying past. He couldn't help but wonder about that Mike Belasko. Was he really CIA or mercenary? Maybe a hired gun from one of the rival right-wing groups that was afraid of the Right Hand of God or who wanted to discredit them. It couldn't be the rich fat cats in Texas who had decided that this was becoming too dangerous for them, sending in some big gun to put a stop to what could threaten to ruin them and their life-styles. Not those guys. He had too much dirt on his sponsors. Hell, they thought like him, wanted the same things he did. Well, if they were, by chance, getting cold feet, Bannon would find out soon enough. If something didn't feel right when those jets landed, Bannon would fly straight to Texas and show his sponsors just what real war and real death looked like. Whatever was happening, something in Bannon's gut told him he hadn't seen or heard the last of Belasko. And something also told him that before they left for either D.C. or Texas plenty of blood was going to be spilled. The big guy was not going to get in their way.

"THAT'S IT from my end. I want you to stay in touch," Brognola told Bolan. "You're definitely onto something. What, exactly, we don't know yet, but it looks bad. And it sure looks like you're getting set to step into some treacherous waters."

"I'm already in up to my neck. I've got a town full of ex-lawmen who have the stench of terrorists all over them. Dirty ex-cops, most likely with the guns to back up their fanaticism. That trooper was murdered for a reason. They had something in that van that would have exposed what I'm realizing is part of some larger scheme."

"I'd say let the state police handle it, but I don't think they'll be able to. You know these guys and how they react—you saw what happened to that trooper. In the meantime, I'll have that delivery made to you at the location you gave me," Brognola said, referring to the M-16 with M-203 grenade launcher Bolan had asked for. He already had the name and a description of the Fed who would make the drop at the rendezvous site, a diner just outside of Pueblo, a location Bolan knew from when he'd come down Highway 78, just before the fateful encounter with Trooper Cowlins. "He'll be waiting to hand it to you personally. Sixteen hundred hours, tomorrow. Your time. You take care."

"I'll be in touch," Bolan said and hung up.

He stayed seated on the edge of the bed, staring at nothing for long moments. He felt grim, troubled, and wondered how to proceed. Should he go to Captain Dawson, lay his suspicions and intel on the man? Let him figure it out and continue to handle the investigation until he dug up something solid? Or hang around, step on some toes, official and unofficial, draw Bannon and the others out, force their hand? As for any known paramilitary groups operating in the state, Brognola had turned up the same hatemongers Dawson had told him about, but nothing on the Right Hand of God Bannon had mentioned. That told Bolan they were either new or that they'd kept themselves out of the mainstream of right-wing paramilitary groups.

With the television off, it was eerily quiet in the room. From outside, there came the occasional sound of a vehicle as it raced down the highway, then there was the silence of the mountain wilderness. There had been nothing about the three men who'd been found executed in the woods or anything about the investigation on the news. Bolan's hunch was that Dawson wanted the media kept on a tight leash so that the state police could proceed with as little interference as possible until they had some concrete proof that all was not well in Honor.

Bolan tried to put the pieces of Brognola's information together. But they were still only jagged edges in a puzzle that was forming an ominous picture. It turned out Hank Maulin was, like one of the men executed in the woods, a former Denver policeman. During his time in the Denver PD, Maulin had received more than a few citizen complaints for excessive force, and there'd been a couple of fatal shootings of suspects, but nothing was ever proved by Internal Affairs. After seven years, Maulin resigned from the PD, and was then somehow elected sheriff of Honor County. *Somehow,* because Bolan suspected the sheriff had brought with him some friends from law enforcement. Money could have changed hands, some intimidation, promises made, and Honor had a new sheriff, quite probably for life. Brognola had also done a computer check on Special Agent Gary Bannon. What Bannon had told Bolan about the incident in the barrio leading to his retirement pretty much played out. Only there were a couple of details Bannon had neglected to mention. One, there was another special agent with Bannon when they had raided the barrio safehouse. The agent's name was Ray Peterson. Whether the two FBI agents had stormed the barrio through the front door or slipped in unnoticed was never determined in the FBI follow-up investigation, although both Bannon and Peterson had claimed they'd gone through the front door and were met by the suspects' gunfire. Another detail Bannon had left out, and one that was played down by the FBI for reasons unknown, was that there were eight alleged self-defense killings of the suspects by Bannon and Peterson. Two of the victims had been women, and one of them had been a fourteen-year-old boy who had later been found to have a .38 revolver on him. So where had the other agents of this task force been? Bolan wondered. Pulled off? Sent in another direction? Had Bannon and Peterson simply been looking to play vigilante heroes, or were they genuinely fed up with the system and had decided to take matters into their own hands? Either way, it looked wrong. Bannon and Peterson had beaten the system they claimed the lawbreakers always defeated and had walked away with the same slap on the wrists. Probably forced into retirement, with the FBI not having enough proof to seek an indictment. So the Feds saved some face, did some damage control and Bannon and Peterson were free to dream up new ways of vigilantism. Only now their death sights were set on any and all so-called "undesirables,'' not to mention the United States government.

Suddenly there was the sound of a powerful engine outside the door. A bright light burned against the curtained window of the room. Bolan killed the nightstand light and drew his .44 Desert Eagle. He moved to the window, staying out of the shafts of light knifing through the window and stretching across the room. He crouched and peered through the blind. It took a moment for him to adjust his eyes to the glaring high beams of the vehicle standing just to the side of his Blazer, but then he caught a shadow behind the truck, holding something bulky. Bolan realized the object in the shadow's hands was a crossbow. His combat senses went on full alert.

Something hit the door with a loud thud. As Bolan unbolted and unchained the door, he heard the gunning of an engine. He surged outside, the hand cannon up and searching for a target. With a squeal of smoking rubber, the truck was already racing down the highway before Bolan could get a good look at the occupants or the license plates.

The soldier holstered the Desert Eagle, then turned and saw what had been left behind. An arrow was impaled in the door, a piece of paper driven through the shaft. Bolan pulled out the arrow, then ripped the paper off the shaft. He grunted when he saw the letterhead of the Right Hand of God, made up of a skull and crossbones over a burning American flag. The articles below were full of the same kind of hate spiel Bannon had put on him earlier. With a quick glance, Bolan could tell that every word had most likely come straight from the mouth of Gary Bannon. The Executioner knew the diatribe: everything was going to hell and anyone who wasn't like them was to blame, and would be the target of their hate and anger, and ultimately their violence. Those who had money, power and authority were also the enemy. They wanted what they had, would spare no one to get it, and they would take it back by whatever means.

Bannon and his ilk were just as guilty of the same wrongs and self-serving motives they accused everyone else who was, in their eyes, undesirable. They preyed on the lowest common human denominator—fear. But Bannon and his cronies were even more guilty and more venomous and dangerous than anyone they sought to destroy, as they spewed their poison. Bannon was sharp and knew how to use words to influence minds, telling followers and would-be followers what they wanted, or believed they wanted, to hear but only in order to further his own twisted visions.

He closed and locked the door behind him. Okay, he thought, snapping the arrow in two and tossing the pieces and the leaflet in the wastebasket, they were warning him—stick around and he'd have to deal with the Right Hand of God.

Well, at least Bolan knew now who the enemy was and that they believed he was some sort of threat to them. And the way Bannon had measured him earlier told Bolan that the ex-Fed suspected he was far more than a Justice Department agent. Bolan was pretty certain that he had gunned down one of the soldiers of the Right Hand of God. Before he left Honor, he intended to take all of them down. Going to Dawson was now out of the question. The captain would most likely demand that Agent Belasko be protected by a cadre of troopers, and the Executioner didn't want his movements encumbered or his motives found out.

And his intent was pure and simple.

Flush out the vipers of Honor and crush them.

Bolan sat on the bed, wondering if he should abandon the motel room. They knew where he was, which made him a sitting target. But he didn't think they would strike at him with such bold and reckless abandon, kicking the door down and coming through with guns blazing. Maybe the phone was tapped, which meant they would know he was in this for the long run. Maybe they would follow him, shadow his every move, waiting to catch him on a desolate stretch of road and cut loose with automatic weapons. Any way it was measured, Bolan knew he would have to be ready for anything the Right Hand of God might throw at him. And they would come at him, he was one-hundred-percent certain of that.

Again, lights hit the curtain and Bolan was off the bed in an eyeblink, the Desert Eagle in hand. A car door banged shut, followed by footsteps, coming right at the door.

As quietly as possible, Bolan unchained and unbolted the door. The footsteps stopped. He grabbed the knob, flung the door open and thrust the Desert Eagle through the opening.

"Good God, man!"

Bolan stared into the bulging eyes of a state trooper. The lawman was no older than twenty-five, but as he pulled his weapon back, Bolan figured the man had just aged about five years.

Bolan leathered the Desert Eagle. "Dawson send you?"

"Yes, sir, he did, as a matter of fact," the trooper said, composing himself. "The captain wanted me to check up on you, to see if everything was all right."

"You can see I'm a little on edge."

"You're damn right I can," the trooper responded.

"If the captain sent you to baby-sit me, tell him I appreciate the gesture, but I don't need my hand held."

The trooper hesitated just enough for Bolan to guess that was one of the reasons for his appearance, but then the lawman went on. "Well, he wanted me to tell you he might not be able to see you tomorrow. He'd like you to stay put, though. Stay here, I mean."

"Tell the captain that if he wants me he can find me in town tomorrow morning."

The trooper started to frown, but nodded, saying, "Have it your way."

Bolan closed the door behind the lawman. Damn, but he was on edge, pumped up on adrenaline like he hadn't been in some time. There were riddles inside of riddles, and he intended to hunt down the answers to all of his questions.

The soldier picked up his Mossberg, jacked the action on the shotgun, then stretched out on the bed.

Tomorrow, he thought. Perhaps it would be the beginning of the end for someone, the beginning of the end to the riddle.

Bolan closed his eyes and tried to sleep.

## 7

Bolan was up at dawn, shaved, showered and was headed out for a recon of Honor County thirty minutes later. The night had passed without further incident. He had slept lightly, just below the level of consciousness, his senses alert for any sound out of the ordinary, his body ready to move at the first hint of danger. As a result, he felt somewhat fatigued and knew he had to have his guard up at all times. To let it slip could prove disastrous. Nothing about Honor and its people, he knew, could be taken at face value. If his suspicions played out, then Bolan intended to tear down Honor's front of quiet small-town America.

With the Desert Eagle and Beretta in their respective holsters, the rifle and shotgun tucked beneath the seat of his Blazer, Bolan spent a couple of hours touring the county. What he found were a lot of backroads, dirt trails and plenty of No Trespassing, Private Property signs. He also spotted mobile homes and shanties in clearings in the woods, with occasional junkyards of abandoned vehicles on vacant lots or in dirt driveways. He began to get the impression that Honor wasn't a very prosperous place to live. Nor, from what he'd learned so far, did Honor County deliver the tranquility promised by the breathtaking beauty of the majestic Rockies that surrounded it. The cloudless sky signaled another day of cool, crisp mountain air and bright sunshine. It was a new day, but Bolan knew it was going to be far from either relaxing or bright. In fact it could be the day that put Honor on the map.

While driving Highway 69 or reconning the paved county roads, Bolan kept an eye on the rearview mirror for a tail. So far, he was alone. Occasionally he passed a state policeman who sat roadside with his cruiser. But there were no roadblocks that morning, no roving police chopper, no sign of a manhunt for those who had executed the men in the woods. Strange, Bolan thought, or had Dawson gotten his man? He was certain the captain either knew about Gary Bannon, Sheriff Maulin and some of the other ex-lawmen of Honor and their suspicious back-

grounds, or would know shortly. Which hopefully would mean a long day spent interrogating
Bannon and his soldiers, with maybe even the
sheriff being put under the microscope by Dawson. That would tie up Bolan's enemies, allowing him to make his rendezvous with Little Joe,
then hit Pueblo to pick up his M-16 rifle with attached grenade launcher.

Bolan found the sign that led to Honor and
took County Road One into town. He entered
Honor from the south on the wide two-lane
paved road that bisected two long stretches of
buildings, and saw a half-dozen Colorado state
police vehicles in parking spots on both sides of
the street. As he made his way to the north end
of the street, beside a large white steepled church,
Bolan discovered even more cruisers and a lot
packed with vehicles of all types. Slowly Bolan
rolled down Main Street. The buildings were a
blend of Old West and modern redbrick and
stucco. Canopied boardwalks stretched in front
of the buildings on both sides of the street. Several of Honor's citizens, most of them male and
the same rough, hard types he'd seen in the saloon the previous night, lounged about or
strolled along the walks. The hostile looks he received told him that the townsmen knew about

the saloon incident and, most likely, knew or had been warned about Agent Mike Belasko and his gunfight with the cop killers on the highway. Bolan didn't think any of the locals would try to flex some muscle again, but he wasn't banking on it.

Bolan reached the end of town about a quarter-mile later. There, the road circled a bronze statue of a frontiersman with a musket. As he rounded the statue, he saw the sheriff's Jeep Cherokee parked in front of a large two-story white building. Cruisers sat next to the vehicle in reserved-for-employees-only slots. A large sign beside the steps declared the building to be the Honor Courthouse.

He recognized one of the vehicles in front of the building as Bannon's Jeep. Okay, the Right Hand of God had been called forth by Dawson to be grilled. Bolan suspected Bannon and his men would survive an intense and thorough interrogation. They were ex-lawmen, after all, and they knew the routine, knew what to say and what not to say. Bannon probably had a litany of alibis and pat answers ready. That alone should flare up suspicion in a seasoned lawman like Dawson. But suspicion might only lead to the war Bolan believed was brewing like thunderclouds over Honor.

Making his way back through the town, Bolan spotted the coffee shop where he was to meet Little Joe and his friend. From the outside, it appeared quaint and typical of small-town America. But there were not the usual pleasant friendly faces of quiet townspeople going about their daily routine. In fact there wasn't much routine at all, but rather a lot of milling around, as men shuffled to and from their vehicles, looking bleary-eyed and seemingly hungover. They looked like trapped animals to Bolan, their expressions both angry and hopeless. Even more the Executioner sensed a distinct feeling of fear hovering over the town, the kind of fear that made a man want to kill just for the hell of it. No, Honor would definitely not be on Bolan's list the next time he sought some R and R.

The soldier found an empty parking slot down from the coffee shop. He killed the engine, got out and locked the door. Making his way up to the boardwalk, he found himself under scrutiny from a group of three men. One of the trio looked about to say something to him, but a state cruiser swung into a parking space in front of them. The trio greeted the lawman with perfunctory nods. The trooper stopped to talk with the men, and Bolan put them out of his mind.

Inside the coffee shop, he found maybe a dozen customers, most of them male and seated at the counter, watching a cable news broadcast, which was turned up loud enough to cover his anticipated talk with Little Joe and the man's friend. Bolan got some curious looks as he made his way to a booth in the farthest corner of the shop and sat down.

A dumpy, blue-haired waitress approached him. "Mornin'," she said. "Wanna hear about the specials?"

"No, thanks. Just coffee," Bolan told her.

He checked his watch. He was five minutes early. Whatever conversation had existed before he'd walked in had died down to a muttered word or a whisper as guys worked on their coffee and breakfast between throwing him the cold eye.

A few minutes later, Little Joe came through the door, accompanied by a blond-haired man in his early forties who was built like a tank: short, but solid, with a granite face and eyes that looked right through one. They were the same kind of cynical but savvy eyes that Bannon had—cop's eyes. Both Little Joe and his companion got the same silent hostility Bolan had received. The two men made their way toward the booth.

"Good morning," Little Joe said brightly. Bolan caught a whiff of whisky on his breath. "Mind if we join you, stranger?"

Up close, Bolan looked at Little Joe's companion, whose shoulders looked ready to burst through his coat. The soldier read the wariness in his blue eyes.

The guy slid into the booth, Little Joe sitting beside him.

"This is Stan Denton," Little Joe said. "Stan, this is the fella who pulled my fat out of the fire last night."

"I heard," Denton said. He grinned at Bolan. "We don't get much quality entertainment around here, but I would have paid to watch you in action last night. The whole county's talking about it."

Bolan studied Denton, who held his stare with a steady but piercing eye. Denton had the same look and tone that Little Joe used as his defense, and, Bolan suspected, the same simmering anger that could erupt if his world was threatened. The Executioner decided he could trust these two men. He read them as the last of a dying breed, men of honor and self-respect, who would go out with a roar on their own terms, and who would stand up and be counted when there was injustice, without shirking from anything or any man. But Little Joe and Denton were there for a reason, and Bolan found himself getting impatient to find out where this was headed.

Little Joe called to the waitress. "A couple of coffees, while we're still young."

The waitress scowled, and Little Joe was treated to some sharp looks from the counter.

"Real friendly town, huh?" Little Joe said to Bolan. "You can tell we're on the outside looking in here, Mr. Belasko. My daughter, by my late wife, is a little beauty who's the spitting image of her mother and who means more to me than anything in the world. Stan's got a nice little ranch where he raises some cattle, and a beautiful Native American wife, to use a politically correct term, who is now carrying a Stan Junior. We're just a couple of guys trying to mind our own business and get through the day." Little Joe turned grim for a moment, then added, "Without getting shot."

Denton's tone was wryly humorous as he said, "Lucky me. The only friend I've got in Honor— a boozer, gambler and smartass. The little scene you had last night, Mr. Belasko, well, I've been there with this guy more times than I care to remember.''

"Hey, come on, Stan. If it weren't for me you'd never have met your second wife." Little Joe grinned at Bolan. "Annie Thundersong is her name. Most beautiful woman you've ever laid eyes on. I mean, to just look at her will bring a tear of pride to your eyes, maybe even make you hate the lucky son of a dog who's married to her."

Bolan sipped at his coffee, then said, "You'll have to excuse me if I keep this short. I've got a busy day ahead of me. If you've got something in mind, or something you want to tell me, I'd like to hear it."

They waited until the waitress brought their coffee.

"I'll pick up the tab," Little Joe said. He dug into his pocket and peeled off a twenty from a wad of bills. "That'll brighten your day a little, good-lookin'," he said to the waitress.

"Don't push it, Joe," she said, but stuffed the twenty into her pocket.

Bolan waited for one of them to speak. Denton took a sip of his coffee, while Little Joe pulled a pint of whiskey from his coat and dumped a splash into his cup.

Denton hunched up close to Bolan, keeping his voice low. "All right, Belasko, I'll get right to it. If you're who I think you are, an agent of the Justice Department, then you could be just the one to bring some real honor to this town. I'm a former trooper of this state. I've lived here for six years since I retired. I know what's going on here. I know there are some dirty former badges calling themselves the Right Hand of God, running loose with dreams of a new America and passing out their hate literature. This used to be a decent town, but now you breathe the air and all you smell is hate, fear and anger. There are more guys around here with automatic weapons than the Colorado state police and a platoon of Green Berets put together. I read you as a man who wants to, or thinks he can, handle business here himself. But you're not alone. Joe and me, we're with you."

Bolan wasn't looking for allies, especially family men who risked leaving heartache behind them.

"Well?" Denton pushed.

Bolan shook his head. "Look . . ." he began.

Denton cut him off, his voice hardening. "You're going to reject our help?"

"This thing is going to turn ugly," Bolan said. "Dawson, as good a cop as he may be, isn't going to get to the truth easily. And if he picks up the stench of what's going on around here, more people are going to die. Both of you have families. You've got something to live for. You've got more going for you that I can see, from just a quick look around, than any man in Honor. Why risk losing it?"

"I understand what you're saying," Denton replied. "But if you think things are that bad, then our lives are at stake either way. In or out of the cross fire. I've held my tongue, looked the other way for too damn long. I've seen the looks they give me and Joe. I've had their hate literature dropped all over my property and my wife threatened. She doesn't even feel safe coming into town anymore. And even when I come in, which I try not to do too often, I've had to choke down my anger when they make their remarks about me or my wife. When I told our good sheriff about all of this, he just shrugged and told me I was the one who had to go and marry a little squaw. That it was my problem. Well, you get the picture. I get the strong feeling they would like me removed.''

Little Joe fished out a cigarette and lit it. ''The two of us talking to you like this already puts our lives in danger. Word will spread. These people are tight, but fear is what holds them together. You corner a mad dog, you had damn well better be ready to kill it. And that's what's here, Belasko. Rabid dogs.

''I found something at their compound this morning,'' Little Joe went on. He glanced over his shoulder but found no one at the counter paying close attention to them. He leaned in toward Bolan and lowered his voice. ''You want to see what that trooper was killed over? Why don't you take a ride with us? Follow us in your vehicle, then, after, if you want to tell us you want to do this alone . . .''

Bolan worked a hard look over Denton and Little Joe, but he knew that neither man was going to say another word until they got what they wanted.

But what they wanted could very well get them killed. Bolan respected both men, and he didn't want their blood on his hands. Still, they made a good argument. In a way, they were like Bannon and his ilk. They wanted life as it used to be, only

Little Joe and Denton wanted peace, not anarchy. The only way they would get peace was to eliminate the source of Honor's hate and fear. They wanted in, but Bolan decided to wait until he saw the reason for Trooper Cowlins's murder before giving them an answer.

"Let's go," he said.

**8**

At the end of the ninety-minute drive west of town, Bolan discovered just how serious Little Joe and Stan Denton were in their desire to team up with him and take down the Right Hand of God.

Locking the door to his Blazer, the soldier stepped out into the narrow clearing that was at the end of a long tortuous uphill drive on a trail just wide enough to allow their vehicles to pass through. With his Mossberg shotgun in hand, Bolan scanned the rocky terrain and surrounding woods as he moved up on Denton's Jeep. Denton and Little Joe stepped out of the vehicle, and Bolan saw that the two men were heavily armed.

Denton and Little Joe looked at Bolan as if daring him to question their need for such firepower. Denton cracked a clip into an AR-18 assault rifle. He was also carrying a holstered .357

Magnum Desert Eagle on his hip. Little Joe canted a FIE SPAS-12 pump autoshotgun to his shoulder, hefting the piece as if it weighed no more than his pint of whiskey. Bolan shook his head, returning Little Joe's wry grin. He didn't even want to ask how they had acquired such firepower. However, given what he had seen and knew about Honor so far, it made sense. These two men, hated outsiders in a town ruled by hate, had loved ones they needed to protect from well-armed fanatics who had already shown Bolan they had the will and the weapons to commit murder.

Little Joe's grin vanished. "This way."

Bolan trailed the two men, his senses primed for any sound or movement in the surrounding woods. They moved up a steep trail that spined the side of the rocky hillside. It was a tough climb along broken ground. Finally they topped the rise to reach a wooded plateau. Fueled by adrenaline and invigorated by the crisp mountain air, Bolan followed Little Joe and Denton for a good ten-minute march through the woods.

At the end of the trail, Bolan saw a lodge in the clearing, which appeared abandoned. Little Joe confirmed Bolan's suspicions that it belonged to the Right Hand of God.

"Right here," the man said, squatting at the side of the narrow trail. He began clearing away some brush while Bolan kept an alert eye on the lodge.

"They've cleared out, there's not a soul there," Little Joe told Bolan, working hard at digging up the sod. "The perimeter was ringed with dozens of bear traps, but I saw they pulled them up and cleaned out their meeting hole. But I'd still watch my step. Took with them all kinds of papers, maps and weapons, too. Inside it's as empty as a tomb, nothing but dust. My guess would be they did that in case the state police decided to take a look around."

"That's a reasonable conclusion," Bolan said. "Again, it confirms they've got something to hide."

"Damn right they do," Little Joe said. "Apart from this morning, when I was here right before dawn, I've been up here a few times before. I've watched them running around with their automatic weapons. I liked to know who they were, where they were and how many. Stan and me, we've got family, after all."

Bolan wanted to tell them that was his whole point, but skipped it, asking instead, "Those the only weapons you have?"

"They are. Why?" Little Joe said.

The soldier shook his head, thinking he might obtain an assault rifle from either Denton or Little Joe and cut out his rendezvous with Brognola's man, save himself the time and remain in Honor just in case it hit the fan. Either way, with the numbers he suspected he might be faced with, Bolan still wanted the grenade launcher and the M-16.

"What about the trail we took in? Do you think Bannon and his pals know about it?" Bolan asked.

"We took the back way in, so I don't think they know about that trail," Little Joe answered.

"But you're not sure."

The man shook his head. "No, not one hundred percent." He removed some more soil, then Bolan saw what looked like an iron door sunk into the ground.

"This," Little Joe said, "is probably why that state policeman was murdered. I saw Bannon and a couple of his flunkies put it in here this morning."

He lifted the iron door, which was on hinges. Bolan stood over Little Joe. There was a good-sized crate in the hole. As the Executioner spotted the US ARMY insignia, Little Joe pulled the top off the crate.

Bolan felt the ice clutch at his stomach. He knelt beside the big man, pulled out and hefted one of the LAW rocket launchers. There were four other LAWs and one MM-1 Multiround Projectile Launcher, which, Bolan knew, was not standard Army issue.

Little Joe had to have read the dark and questioning concern in Bolan's eyes because he said, "Why would they need this kind of firepower?"

Denton spoke for the first time. "I say we take it, see what Bannon does."

"We'll take it, all right," Bolan said, standing. "But we'll put it in my vehicle. When Bannon finds his toys missing, I'm betting he'll come after me."

"Then what?" Denton asked. "The guy has this kind of firepower for a reason. What's to say this is the only crate of LAWs he has laying around? If that's the case, he might not even miss a few launchers."

"Oh, he'll miss it," Bolan said. "Bannon doesn't strike me as the kind of man who likes to have anything taken from him. I have a feeling he'll sweat when he finds this crate gone."

"Who knows what he has in mind?" Denton went on. "Hell, he may be looking to blow up the whole goddamn town. I read Bannon and the others as crazy enough to do just that."

Bolan's gaze narrowed. "I don't think that's part of his game plan."

He turned to address Little Joe. "You say you've seen maps when you were here before, Joe?"

"Yeah, tacked up on the walls, and such. Basic maps, most of them. Colorado, Kansas, Oklahoma, one of Missouri. Maybe they have other branches there. Maybe they're looking for locations to set up new branches. I don't know. But there was this one map of Virginia and a map of Washington, D.C., in particular I found strange."

Alarm bells began to sound in Bolan's head.

"Go on," he prodded.

"Pennsylvania Avenue was all marked off in red," Little Joe answered. "They had the White House circled in red, too, with small *X*s crossed through different locations of the White House. There were a couple of other areas on the map marked off, looked like two places somewhere else in town."

"Do you know what these places were or on what streets they were located?"

The man shook his head. "No, but it seemed like they were quite close to the White House. The time I got inside the lodge, I only got a quick look at the maps. Someone drove up, and I moved out. There wasn't much time to look at the map of Virginia, either, but it looked like they had an area, maybe thirty, forty miles west of Washington marked off."

Bolan tried to digest this information, but all he was coming up with were new questions with new and even more insidious implications and no bona fide answers. The only thing he could be reasonably certain of was that the killers of Trooper Cowlins had been transporting the crate of rocket launchers due to be delivered to Bannon. The three killers had rendezvoused with Bannon, dropped the hardware, then Bannon had executed them. A seriously wounded man, bleeding all over the place, was a liability, and Bannon needed to sever any link between himself and three soldiers who had gunned down a state policeman. Bolan also knew that Denton had made a good point—there was a strong possibility that Bannon had more LAWs stashed away, anywhere in the rugged, trackless wilderness of the Rockies. No, Bolan didn't like it one damn bit.

There was no way he could dismiss the ominous feeling that he was onto some horrific scheme Bannon had been planning for some time and was getting ready to put into motion. Bolan was betting his life there was some connection between the rocket firepower and the marked-up map of D.C. And if what Bolan was thinking turned out to be true, then Bannon was planning on taking a trip to 1600 Pennsylvania Avenue. Anybody in their right mind would consider it a suicide mission, but Bolan knew skilled and determined savages could pull off a grandstand attack on the White House.

As Bolan helped Little Joe haul out the crate, the sound of a powerful engine came from the direction of the lodge. Combat senses flaring, the Executioner moved up the trail a bit and crouched beside an aspen. Roaring off the trail near the lodge was a black Jeep.

"Get that crate out of here!" Bolan called over his shoulder to Little Joe and Denton. The two men hesitated, looking as if they intended to drop their load and fight instead.

"Move it!" Bolan ordered.

The Jeep stopped, and Bolan spotted two figures in the vehicle. A moment later, he recognized Ray Peterson in the driver's seat. The distance was too great for the shotgun to be effective, so Bolan unleathered the Desert Eagle. But just as he got off a shot, the Jeep whipped into reverse, kicking up a funnel of dust. The Right Hand of God soldiers secured cover.

Bolan looked around and saw Little Joe and Denton hauling the crate down the trail. Suddenly autofire rang out, shaving off the tree bark next to Bolan's head. He threw himself against the slender aspen, as bullets raked the trail, then chanced a look around the corner. Peterson and another Right Hand of God hardman were crouched behind the trees in the distance. Bolan triggered the Desert Eagle three times, drilling .44 slugs into Peterson's tree cover. The other hate-monger popped up and cut loose with an M-16. Bolan scanned the area for their Jeep, wanting to disable the vehicle, hoping then to move in on the ex-lawmen. He needed a prisoner, wanted answers from them any way he could get them, but he saw he wasn't going to get the chance to take the fight to the enemy.

Firing wildly with their assault rifles, they forced Bolan to hug the aspen as rounds tore off the tree bark and shredded brush. The Executioner waited for a lull in the firing to move out and in. It came a second later when he heard the vehicle's engine start up. Sliding out onto the trail, Bolan watched as a dust cloud boiled in the distance. Then the rev of the engine pealed over the clearing before slowly fading.

Bolan sprinted down the trail and caught up with Denton and Little Joe, covering their backs as they retreated with the crate on their shoulders.

"If there's a welcoming reception waiting for us down that gulley, drop the crate and help me show them what you've got," Bolan said.

Little Joe threw him a grin over his shoulder.

"Yes," the soldier said, "you're in."

The Executioner knew the war in Honor had begun, and the three of them were high on the Right Hand of God's list of targets.


"THEY WHAT?" Bannon snarled into his portable phone, the fury burning hot and strong inside him. "Don't say anything more over the phone," he ordered Peterson. "You know the contingency plan we talked about this morning? Do it. Get back here as soon as it's done. I'll be sending out another team. Don't try to contact me again until it's done."

Bannon killed the communication and flung the phone on the table that was littered with their war maps. He felt the eyes of his soldiers boring into him, but he didn't meet their gazes.

Damn it, it was all going to hell, he thought. Everything in his life, from two failed marriages, to his forced retirement from the FBI, had gone to hell just when he was about to turn the corner and make it big. Only this time, he could not fail in his supreme mission to put America back on the road to glory and morality. He would summon all his strength, skill and furious determination to kill anyone and everyone who stood in his way. Bannon knew he had men, real men, with him who thought and felt the same as he did, and who had the strength and boldness to act.

"What's wrong?"

He turned slowly at the sound of Tom Barker's voice. Two dozen soldiers were crammed into the living room of the mobile home. All of them were watching him, Bannon saw, and waiting. He read the grim anxiety in their stares, smelled the fear in the room, but he knew they were all ready to go. Damn right, they knew the deal. They had accepted the risks in order to gain their reward at the end of the line, had pledged their loyalty to the death to the movement, sworn to one another no betrayal, no retreat and no surrender, even if they had to go out facing down an army of police. They were too close, had come too far to abort their mission. Everything had been laid out, from Operation Whitewater Death to Operation Honor Armageddon, but only a select number of his men knew the full and final details simply because he didn't trust everyone in the movement. Everything was set to go—except now Bannon had three major hurdles in his way—Mike Belasko, the Indian and Stan Denton.

Bannon didn't answer Barker right away. Instead, he let his eyes take in the room. With the exception of Wilkins and two of his former Army buddies, Hodges and Sterling, they were all ex-lawmen of some sort, ranging from city cops to ex-FBI and Secret Service agents. Paulson and Martin, two former Dallas policemen who had been thrown off the force after gunning down a couple of teenaged crack dealers. There was Bitman and Corrals, Arizona state troopers who were also forced into early retirement because they wouldn't apologize for what the media had called their racist-fascist police state views when all they'd done was speak the truth.

As Bannon looked around at his followers, it struck him, more than ever before, that all of them had one thing in common. They had all been forced to retreat from a world that didn't have the guts to stomach the truth. But the movement was ready to come out of the shadows and blaze a new age, and it was going to start with the obliteration of 1600 Pennsylvania Avenue.

Bannon recalled how he'd shaped the Right Hand of God. What had started out as bull sessions with a few former cops over war stories had branched out by word of mouth and the justifiable anger of men forced to the edge, where soon Bannon had formed a small army. Each and every one of them were men who knew they had to do something about the madness swirling around them, thanks mostly to those holding the reins of power in Washington.

Bannon addressed his soldiers. "We've got problems. Peterson just saw the Fed, the Indian and Denton running off with some of our firepower."

He got a strong reaction from his men, read the rage in their eyes.

"They'll go right to Dawson," Corrals said.

"No, I don't think so," Bannon replied. "Dawson tried to shake our trees this morning, and he came up with zero. You guys all held up. I'm damn proud of you men for staying hard. Before I got this news from Peterson, our good friend, Sheriff Maulin, called and told me Dawson and his boys had pulled out. The captain thinks he has a whiff of something suspicious, but he doesn't have anything solid. He'll be back to pick our brains with some more Q and A, but by then we'll be gone. Right now, it's us and them. The town of Honor, as well as those three guys who grabbed our rocket launchers, are on their own.

"All right. Here's what we've got. Our tap on Belasko's phone tells us he's meeting with another Fed outside Pueblo in a few hours to pick up some additional firepower. Barker, you told me you know the place." As the man nodded, Bannon went on. "Okay. Take seven men with you. I want Belasko out of the picture permanently. All I want to see on the news tonight are two dead Feds in body bags. And if it means eliminating all witnesses, well, that's just too damn bad for them. If Belasko thinks he can handle us on his own, he needs to be taught the ultimate lesson. And I want my merchandise back. We've got too much riding on this to bail out now. Whoever gets in our way will have to be destroyed.''

Paulson spoke up. ''If it's a lock, and we're set to go with the others at the state line, is it smart to snatch the Indian's kid and Denton's squaw?''

Bannon bared his teeth. ''I don't like having anything taken from me. I always knew the Indian and Denton, who never had the guts to be one of us, would someday become thorns in my side. That day has arrived. The three of them, as Peterson told me, are heavily armed. Meaning they want a fight. Meaning they have to go down and stay down. That's why I laid out my plan this morning to snatch their women. They're insurance, in case the heat put our backs to the wall. I know, we've got other LAWs and the explosives stashed away, and another shipment came in this morning, but I'll be damned if I'll let them get away with taking my merchandise. If it comes to turning this county into a mass graveyard with all of their bones, it will be done. Our way is the only way. Any more questions before we get on with it?''

Bannon watched them nodding in agreement. They wanted the same things he did—power, wealth and changes in the system—possible only through anarchy and violence. Besides, all of them knew that the day would come when it was time to put into action all the talk about revolution. They were at the threshold, Bannon knew, of change. Nothing was going to get in the way of the Right Hand of God and his personal greatness and gain.

Bannon observed his soldiers pick up M-16s or shotguns, a hungry look in their eyes.

Barker pumped the action on his Ithaca 37 shotgun as he said to Bannon, "Try and catch the news tonight, Chief."

BOLAN BOUNCED the Blazer off the trail, swerved into the shoulder of Highway 17, then stopped. They had seen no more of the enemy during the thirty-minute retreat from the mountain compound, but he wasn't taking any chances. He searched the highway in both directions as he got out, ready to pull the Desert Eagle if the enemy came roaring up. The crate with Bannon's rocket power was in the back of the truck and would stay there. If and when he was stopped by the real police, he might have to use Brognola's clout. Or he might have to come clean with Dawson. Either way, Bolan hoped it wouldn't become a showdown of wills with the state or local police. Dawson might be the law, but at this point the soldier knew every side was on its own.

Bolan walked up to Denton and Little Joe, who had slid in behind his vehicle. "I have someplace I need to be." He gave them his room number at the motel, saying, "I'll be back no later than eight. Be there. Don't stay out front if I'm not back. Take a drive around instead." He caught the flicker of concern in their eyes. "You wanted in, you're in. In the meantime, get your women and take them far away from Honor County before we meet again."

"Bannon's crazy, but he's not stupid," Denton said. "If he comes after our families that will start a war."

"I believe he's crazy enough to do just that," Bolan told the two men. "This guy is going for broke. A man who kills his own people because they became a liability won't stop until everyone he hates or is a threat to him is dead. Or he winds up dead."

"We'll be there," Little Joe told Bolan.

The Executioner felt a momentary pang. There was no turning back for Denton and Little Joe. The enemy knew their faces and wanted a piece of them.

Bolan got into his Blazer and roared off to keep his meet with Brognola's man.

**9**

The detour to the Right Hand of God's compound had cost Bolan valuable time, making him late for his rendezvous with Brognola's man. Already, the soldier was counting down the doomsday numbers in his head, grimly aware that Judgment Day was close for the former lawmen who had jumped to the other side of the tracks.

Bolan tried to shake the ice ball of dread lodged in his gut, the sixth sense burning a steady flow of adrenaline through his veins.

What bothered Bolan as much as anything was the fact that he had unwillingly taken on allies. The last thing he wanted was the blood of two good and innocent men and their families on his hands. Knowing the kind of man Bannon was, Bolan feared that the Right Hand of God would try to go after Little Joe and Denton and their loved ones before he had a chance to get back to Honor.

He tried to will that disturbing thought out of his mind as he drove toward his rendezvous. He kept himself on high alert, searching the highway for any sign of a tail. Earlier, he had spotted a vehicle keeping pace with him, but staying back about a hundred yards. Finally, just when he'd been about to pull over and let the truck pass, it had slowed and cut down a side road.

After a while, Bolan spotted the diner off to the side of the road in the distance. He took the winding dirt road to the diner, checking his rear- and sideview mirrors, but saw nothing other than a spool of dust he left behind and a deserted roadway in both directions.

The isolated diner was a good-sized wooden building with a canopied boardwalk and large plate-glass windows on either side of the front door. It sat perched out in the middle of nowhere, dwarfed by the snowcapped ridges of the looming Rockies. Only the telephone lines running from the diner and strung off toward the highway by a series of wooden poles seemed to link it to civilization. With the sun beginning to lower behind the jagged teeth of the Rockies, casting shadows over the valley, it felt eerie to

Bolan. Still, it was the same place he had stopped to eat before his fateful rendezvous with violent death in Honor County.

Bolan counted a half dozen vehicles parked out front, including a black four-door Plymouth. Swinging around three gas pumps, the soldier parked his vehicle on the passenger's side of the Plymouth. He killed the engine, then made eye contact with the man behind the sedan's wheel. Brognola's man stepped out of the car. He was a tall, lean man with a sharp chiseled face, dressed in a black leather jacket and gray pants. After detecting the bulge of a holstered weapon beneath the man's coat, Bolan got out.

"I'm Agent Chambers, Mr. Belasko. I'm assuming you'd like to see some ID?"

"No need. You're either who you are or you're not."

The agent chuckled. "Right. Brognola said to skip any code words or funny handshakes. Told me you're not one for secret-agent games."

"I'm afraid this isn't any game, Agent Chambers," Bolan commented.

"By the looks of what I picked up for you, I would say not," Chambers said as he opened the trunk of the car. He gestured toward the large black satchel in the trunk. "Everything you wanted. One M-16 rifle with twenty spare clips. Six 40-mm grenades for the M-203 grenade launcher. There's also blacksuit, webbing and pouches in the bag."

Bolan hauled out the satchel. "I appreciate your promptness and efficiency."

Chambers shut the trunk. "No problem."

Bolan went to his Blazer, opened the door and put the satchel on the floor on the passenger's side.

"It's been a long ride," Bolan heard Chambers begin to say, when suddenly his attention was drawn to two vehicles slowly rolling down the highway, heading toward the diner. Bolan was certain one of the vehicles was the truck that had turned off the road earlier.

"If you'd like to join me, I'm going to grab a bite before I head back to Denver," Chambers finished.

Bolan picked up his fully loaded Mossberg shotgun, then zipped open his duffel bag and took out a dozen spare 12-gauge shells and stuffed them into his coat pocket. Locking the car door, he turned to the Justice agent.

"A quick bite would be fine. I need to call Brognola anyway," Bolan said, wanting to in-form the big Fed of what he had learned of a possible attack on the White House. "What kind of piece do you have under your coat?"

"A 9 mm Glock." The agent scanned the perimeter of the diner. "You expecting company, Belasko?"

"I'm not sure. Could be." Bolan jacked the shotgun's action, chambering the first of the Mossberg's eight 12-gauge rounds. "You might want to be ready to flash your ID. I don't want anybody to think I've come to rob the place. Do you have a quarter?"

Chambers dug into his pocket and handed Bolan a quarter for his collect call to Brognola. On the way up the steps to the boardwalk, the Executioner looked over his shoulder. He saw that the two vehicles had stopped on the shoulder of the road. The hairs rose on the back of his neck. He was being watched, he was sure of it.

Agent Chambers followed Bolan's stare toward the highway.

"How come I get the feeling you're going to tell me you were followed?" Chambers asked. When Bolan didn't answer right away, he added, "Maybe you want to fill me in on anything I need to know."

"Just keep your eyes peeled and your hand close to that Glock," Bolan replied shortly.

Inside the diner, the soldier was met with expressions of alarm as the customers locked on the shotgun he held by his side. A big beefy man in a stained apron growled from behind the counter, "Hey, what's going on?"

Agent Chambers already had out his ID. "Relax. We're both agents of the Department of Justice."

"If you don't mind, pal, I'd like to take a little closer look at that ID," the beefy guy said. From the man's tone, Bolan suspected he probably kept some fairly serious hardware underneath the counter within easy reach.

"No problem," Chambers replied, moving toward the counter.

There were booths against the walls on both sides of the large room, with a few round tables in the middle of the floor. The high wooden counter stretched along the entire length of the back wall. Glass cases holding cakes and doughnuts lined the counter, with a series of glass coolers, stuffed with beer and perishables situated behind the counter. A dozen coffeepots and two soda machines flanked the coolers. A jukebox against the wall at one end of the counter was softly playing a country-and-western song. Bolan got the impression that this out-of-the-way diner was braced for a rush of customers it would never get unless an army of Hell's Angels or a convoy of eighteen-wheelers rolled in.

With the eyes of the patrons and the waitresses following him, Bolan angled toward the pay phone on the wall at the end of the counter. He saw the beefy guy give Chambers's ID a thorough eyeballing before grunting his acceptance of the situation. Chambers then took a seat at the opposite end of the counter from Bolan, and ordered coffee. Two old-timers working on sandwiches and a large pitcher of beer sat next to the justice man.

Bolan leaned his shotgun against the wall. He had his hand on the phone receiver when he heard the rumbling of engines and doors slamming outside. Bolan turned and looked through the plate-glass window, where he saw at least a half-dozen men had disgorged from two vehicles and were making their way along the boardwalk. Even with the dust thrown up by the idling vehicles, the Executioner could make out four figures armed with either shotguns or assault rifles.

The first three hardmen burst through the door of the diner, weapons poised. As Bolan grabbed his shotgun, they swung their weapons toward him and opened fire. More gunmen surged through the doorway, fanning out and cutting loose with their weapons. Screams began to lance the air over the thunder of shotguns and the blister of autofire. Bolan darted for cover behind the counter, the phone he'd been about to use exploding under the barrage of weapons' fire. He couldn't tell exactly how many of the enemy he was faced with, but going by the fire that was obliterating the glass cases and shearing chunks off the counter over his head, Bolan estimated there were about six heavily armed men.

Bolan was now certain that his phone had been tapped, allowing Bannon's soldiers to track him to the diner. Worse, this frontal assault told him they were not only determined to take out Agent Mike Belasko, but they weren't about to leave any witnesses behind. Bolan hadn't anticipated such an attack, especially in a public place. Clearly Bannon was going all the way, and the ex-FBI agent didn't care who or how many he killed. Silently Bolan cursed himself for being caught off-guard and risking innocent lives. But it was too late for hindsight, and the soldier knew he had to throw it back in the face of the enemy or he, Chambers and everyone else in that diner would die.

Under a barrage of detonating glass and flying liquids from the coolers, Bolan crawled several yards up the counter. Suddenly Chambers came rolling over the top. He crashed to the floor, his 9 mm Glock still in his hands. He appeared unharmed and ready to fight.

The storm of buckshot and bullets continued to decimate the counter and coolers in a seemingly endless and deafening cacophony of fire. Beyond the counter, Bolan could hear the crash of tables and the thud of bodies, while screams rent the air.

The soldier checked the rear—just in time to see a wild-eyed hardman with an M-16 rifle pop around the corner of the counter. Braving the hurricane of glass and wood shards, Bolan almost sawed the guy in two with a shotgun blast to the stomach that kicked the disemboweled man into the wall, leaving it smeared with blood. Out of the corner of his eye, Bolan then caught sight of a figure with an assault rifle bounding onto the counter, midway down. Tracking on with his Mossberg, the Executioner triggered his message of doom at the same instant Chambers cored several 9 mm bullets into the guy. With an eruption of spurting gore and shredded cloth, the man was launched from the counter as if he'd just stepped on a grenade.

With the sound of fresh clips being slapped into assault rifles, the merciless assault on the counter resumed. There was no way, with bullets and buckshot tearing up the counter and ripping gaping holes into the wall behind him, that Bolan could lift his head and start selecting targets. The way they kept pounding his position and the rest of the counter with sweeping streams of fire, he knew they were spread out and hoping to either flush him out or catch him with a lucky round. Bolan needed an evasive tactical maneuver.

He found one.

A blast of shotgun fire shattered a wooden door at the end of the counter that seemed to lead to the kitchen. Jerking his head at Chambers toward the devastated opening, Bolan kept low as he bolted through the jagged shards of wood, Chambers right on his heels. They found themselves in a small kitchen. Judging from the way the enemy kept firing at the counter, Bolan knew they hadn't seen them dart into the kitchen.

"Like I said before," Chambers gasped, "you want to tell me anything I need to know?"

Bolan spotted a narrow hall that led to the back door. "After. Come on," the soldier said, swiftly leading the way down the hall and out the back door, the heavy-metal thunder of weapons' fire raging behind them.

They carefully rounded the corner of the building, but the boardwalk in front of the diner was empty. Bolan reloaded the Mossberg. Suddenly there was silence, with the only sound the wailing of a female singer coming from the jukebox. Then a shotgun blast rang out, followed by the shattering of glass and the singing stopped. Bolan waited, his senses straining. He saw faint wisps of gunsmoke drift through the open door of the diner and heard the sound of footsteps crunching over broken glass.

Bolan wiped away the streaks of blood from the superficial cuts on his face caused by flying glass.

"He's not here," he heard a man say from inside the diner.

"If you're in the back, I strongly urge you and the other guy with you to come out with your hands up," another voice said.

"Do you hear me, Belasko?" the voice went on when there was no response. "Nobody here has died—yet. The owner here, he tried to play hero and pulled a shotgun. But he only took one through the shoulder. He'll live. But if you want, I can start killing these people, one by one, until you come out. I think you know the deal."

Bolan knew the deal, all right. It was all or nothing. He gave Chambers a grim look, nodded and handed the man his Beretta, the Glock filling the Justice man's other hand.

The soldier quickly laid out his attack plan. It wasn't fancy, but everything was bold—in through the front door, move away from each other and start blasting. Only the quickest and the meanest gun would survive. Bolan intended to survive.

The guy who had urged Bolan to give up began yelling that they had ten seconds left. As the guy began counting down the doomsday numbers, Bolan crouched below the plate-glass window and edged his way toward the open door.

A figure armed with an assault rifle showed on the side of the window. The Executioner made his move. He triggered the shotgun, blowing a tidal wave of glass over the hardman. The guy dropped to the floor, minus his head.

Bolan surged into the diner in the next heartbeat. He took in the numbers, counting five hardmen spread out over the room. As he had hoped, the enemy was frozen for a critical moment by the sight of one of their number going down. It also helped that a couple of hardmen in Bolan's immediate kill radius were reloading shotguns or slamming fresh clips into their assault rifles. He used the delay to killing advantage.

Jacking the shotgun's pump action, he whirled and launched a man across the diner with a 12-gauge explosion that tunneled open the guy's chest. Peeling off to the warrior's flank, Chambers began blasting double-fisted messages of doom with the Beretta and Glock. He slid away from the sudden return fire that blew out the other plate-glass window, as Bolan pumped the Mossberg, tracking on for a big guy at the counter armed with an Ithaca shotgun. As the hardman started to swing his weapon toward Bolan, the warrior fired, the 12-gauge round catching the enemy high in the chest and flinging him like a rag doll over the counter. Bolan turned his grim death sights elsewhere. Three of Bannon's soldiers at the far end of the counter were firing wildly with stammering M-16s, aware that their fellows were dying hard and quick. As a raging hornet's nest of 5.56 mm lead began tattooing the floor in front of Bolan, he darted to the side. Another blast from the Mossberg blew up a huge chunk of counter in front of the trio of gunmen.

Downrange from the Executioner, Chambers punched double-fisted death into one of the hardmen, the 9 mm slugs marching up his chest and into his side, causing him to spin and topple facedown into the glass teeth of the jukebox.

Bolan held his ground, pumping and firing at the remaining hardmen who were ducking the tidal wave of shotgun blasts ripping off chunks of the counter, before popping up and spraying the room with autofire. When the Executioner had expended the final round of his shotgun, he drew his Desert Eagle, and not a second too soon.

The hardman Bolan had blasted over the counter suddenly staggered to his feet. Drenched in blood, and with a savage snarl on his lips, the guy lifted the Ithaca with shaking hands. Bolan brought up the .44 and shot the guy in the face at almost point-blank range, all but decapitating him.

He saw that Chambers was coming under intense return fire. Then the Justice agent dived into a booth that took him out of the direct line of fire. In the next instant it became clear to Bolan that the surviving enemy was more intent on flight than fight. Two fanatics burst from cover, triggering their assault rifles in wild, sweeping sprays. Bolan was forced to duck behind the edge of the counter as slugs bit off wood above his head. Crouching, he crawled around the corner, while Chambers bolted to his feet and began to drill slugs into a hardman's chest. As the Justice man's target toppled, the hand cannon in Bolan's fist thundered, but the .44 round only blasted off a piece of hanging glass as the last fanatic leaped through the shattered window.

Bolan heard someone groan behind him. He turned around to see the diner's owner slumped against the wall. His apron was bloody, and he held one hand clamped over his shoulder. The guy would live, Bolan could tell. But then he heard a car door slam and knew it wasn't over yet.

Quickly holstering his Desert Eagle, the soldier reloaded his shotgun and moved toward the shattered window. With the sound of an engine gunning to life, he stepped through the opening and chambered a 12-gauge round. The surviving hardman caught sight of Bolan. He stuck an M-16 through the window and triggered a short burst that forced the Executioner to bolt across the boardwalk as the 5.56 mm slugs ripped up the planks.

The enemy threw the Jeep Cherokee into reverse, kicking up a cloud of dust.

Bolan bounded off the walk to turn up the heat, the Mossberg roaring in his fist. The hardman had to have seen it coming, because he ducked a heartbeat before the windshield was blown to pieces over his head. Angling out into the lot, Bolan jacked the pump action, as he cut the gap to the man's vehicle.

The hardman hit the gas again, whipping his vehicle farther back before sluicing it around. Bolan moved ahead, ripping the hood off the Jeep with another blast of the Mossberg.

Then he went for the gas tank.

As the Jeep's tires grabbed at dirt, the Executioner fired, pumped, then fired again, riddling the side of the vehicle with gaping holes. Walking on through the swirling wall of dust, he kept pumping and triggering the shotgun. Each 12-gauge blast thudded into the vehicle with such force that it threatened to put the Jeep on its side.

On the eighth and final blast, Bolan struck explosive pay dirt.

The fireball shredded the Jeep, hurling wreckage across the lot. The vehicle had to have had close to a full tank, because the blast was tremendous, lifting the hull off the ground and hurling it into the air before crashing it onto its roof.

The Executioner held his ground as raging flames crackled around the Jeep.

Suddenly a bone-chilling scream ripped the air, as a shrieking flaming figure rolled from the fiery wreck. Bolan drew his Desert Eagle and put a round through the hardman's chest, kicking him off his feet as if he'd been hit by a wrecking ball.

For long moments, the only sounds were the flames licking around the Jeep and the rasping breath of Agent Chambers, who'd exited the diner at a run.

"I've got a live one inside," the agent told Bolan. "The guy was wearing a vest."

"Sounds like a man who wants to keep on living," he said, knowing he had just found his prisoner. "Did you see anybody other than the owner hurt?"

"No. Just the bad guys, and they're hurt in the worst possible way."

"I need some time, Chambers. Twelve hours, maybe less. Can you keep these people here? And if the state police show up, can you keep them off my back?"

Chambers frowned. "What you're asking would certainly buck all department procedure. I don't know if I can."

"Can you try?" Bolan asked.

"I'll call Brognola. If I have to, I can get a team of agents here within an hour to keep this situation under control. But I can't make any promises. What do you have in mind?"

"I'm going hunting."

Chambers handed Bolan his Beretta. "In that case, you might want this back."

**10**

Mack Bolan figured he was only thirty minutes outside the Honor County line, but it felt like an eternity separated it from the carnage left behind at the diner. Keeping a constant eye out for flashing lights, or worse, another vehicle full of Bannon's soldiers, he stuck to the speed limit, as the fingers of twilight stretched over the mountain country.

After filling Chambers in on Bannon and his right-wing paramilitary group, the Justice man had promised to keep the situation at the diner under control, not letting anyone leave, or if anyone came onto the premises, keeping them there. Before heading out, Bolan had put in a call to Brognola, using Chambers's cellular car phone. The big Fed was sending a team of agents to the diner to help calm down and make sure the patrons and employees stayed put, which would give Bolan either enough time to hunt down the enemy, or hang himself. Brognola had vowed to flex some muscle with the state or local police if he had to and override their authority. But if Dawson picked up the scent of the slaughter— and Bolan knew that sooner or later he would— then it was highly likely that the big trooper would try to put Bolan on a tight leash so he could go after Bannon by legal means.

At this point, the soldier knew that bringing in Bannon and his soldiers cuffed, and with their rights read, was impossible. The mere thought of the man, what he had been, done, created, and worse, what he intended to do, knotted Bolan's guts. One of the worst kinds of savages in the Executioner's view was a dirty cop, someone who had sworn to uphold the law, to defend and protect the innocent, but who had tossed away their badge, their duty and their honor for personal gain. As ex-cops, Bolan knew the last thing Bannon and his comrades wanted was a trip down any maximum-security cellblock. Prison would most certainly prove a fate worse than death. No, they would go down fighting and they would go out hard, taking anything and anyone with them.

It didn't help that Bolan's own legal situation might have become tenuous, with him walking a fine line between state and federal jurisdiction in his battle against the Right Hand of God. Even though they had been clear self-defense killings, Bolan suspected Dawson would be frothing mad over what he would probably consider "cowboy play" by Agent Belasko. Bolan only hoped the man would not put him in a position where he'd have to throw down his weapons and butt out. If that happened, the soldier would comply with the full letter of the law and let Brognola bail him out or put him back in the hunt.

He glanced at his prisoner who wore the frightened look of a cornered ferret. Bolan recognized him as one of Bannon's cohorts who had come calling on him the night before at the motel. The guy had identified himself as Wilkins. He now sat slumped against the door, still wearing the bulletproof vest that had absorbed the brunt of Chambers's 9 mm barrage. Wilkins was lucky, Bolan thought, but his luck would hold only as long as he made himself useful. So far, he hadn't told Bolan much more than that he was ex-Army and had been wanting out of the clutches of the Right Hand of God for some time.

Bolan picked up the blood-spotted towel that lay beside him and dabbed at the gashes on his forehead and scalp. Back at the diner it had taken the soldier a little longer than he would have liked to get the blood to stop seeping from his cuts and scratches and to pick the glass out of his hair. With the adrenaline still pumping through his veins, pain wasn't a problem at the moment, but any trickle of blood could prove a nuisance if it ran into his eyes. He stemmed the blood and dumped the towel on the seat beside himself and his prisoner.

"Let's go over what you've told me," Bolan said.

Wilkins heaved a breath. "Look, I already told you everything I know. What more do you want from me?"

"Answers. I get the feeling you're holding back."

"Bannon never let me in on the final details of the attack on the White House. I told you. He didn't trust me. The way it looks now, I get the feeling he sent me with the others as some kind of sacrificial lamb."

"If that's the case, you beat him. But if you want to keep on breathing, you'll give me more than what you have," the Executioner said.

Wilkins seemed to think hard about something, and it was a long moment before he replied. "All I know is they're leaving some time tonight. There's a crew, another chapter of the movement, ready to link up with Bannon."

"How many? And where?"

"At one of the briefings I heard there were twenty, could be as many as thirty. I think they're coming in from Kansas and going to rendezvous tonight with Bannon. It's supposed to happen at the state line, but Bannon could have bumped up the timetable or made the rendezvous closer to home after what's happened. Anyway, I know the route they planned to take to the fly site."

"There's a map of the state and a pen in the glove box. Before we get back, I want you to outline the route."

"What is it you plan on doing with me? If I'm helping you—"

"Your continued existence is riding on your helping me," Bolan said, cutting him short. "Now, how do they plan to get to the East Coast?"

"They fly out in Lear jets, a half dozen of them, to be exact, bound for their attack on the White House. Complete with antiradar, antitracking equipment. Bannon's whole operation is well-organized and it's heavily financed. But he needs money to, uh, keep the dream alive. This operation, his first mission, as he calls it, has cost him just about every dollar he has.''

Bolan gave the guy a questioning look. ''You seem to know a lot for a guy who isn't trusted.''

''If nothing else, I know how to survive,'' Wilkins said. ''I kept my ears opened. I knew how to play Bannon's game.''

''The kind of transportation you're talking about takes money.''

''Bannon has the money. So do a lot of the others in the movement. They've got connections, contacts in the military, guys with money and clout you wouldn't even suspect would have anything to do with a bunch of nuts like Bannon and his ex-cop buddies. I was one of those Army connections he used to get his hands on those LAWs. Then he started grooming some other sources along the way. That's when I got the feeling I was expendable. What you don't know is that Bannon ran guns, a lot of guns, to inner city gangs for a few years. Money from those guns provided the capital to form the Right Hand of God. How about that, huh? The same people he despises he's done business with. Only the way he talks about it, he figures he's only helping to rid society of undesirables. Bannon cashes in, while hoping a lot of undesirables cash each other out. You're a Fed, you know the deal. The gun business is booming in the cities.''

Bolan clenched his jaw. The more he heard about the ex-Fed, the more he knew Bannon needed to be taken out. But it was going to be a tough battle yet. Bolan had seen the face of hate and rage many times before, but recalling the look in Bannon's eyes had been a new and chilling experience even for him. Like all fanatics, Bannon actually believed in his twisted cause, that he was right and everyone else was wrong, that he could make the world a better place in which to live. But Bannon's intention was to dominate and control, to call the shots by killing anyone who didn't think, or who was not, like him.

Damn right, the worst was yet to come. When he returned to Honor, Bolan knew he would be facing a small army of well-armed fanatics who thought and felt the same way as Bannon. Maybe the entire town of Honor was pulling for Bannon, for all he knew. From what Wilkins had already told him, Bolan knew the odds were stacked against him. With forty or more hardmen to deal with, he was all too glad he now had the additional firepower of the M-16 with attached grenade launcher. Not to mention what he'd taken from Bannon.

"So, you're telling me Bannon has clout in high places?" Bolan prompted Wilkins to continue.

"He calls them his sponsors. After he was pretty much kicked out of the FBI, there were a few guys in suits in Texas that Bannon either knew or had something on. At first they were Bannon's drinking buddies, who liked to play at being weekend warriors, you know, thinking it made them renegades or tough guys, to run with radical ex-cops in Dallas. Then I guess they liked what Bannon was saying about America and its decline. So they funneled some money to Bannon to help him get his organization off the ground, but they were content to watch from the sidelines. I don't think these guys were aware of Bannon's moonlighting as a gunrunner, or they might have gotten cold feet."

"You have any names of these so-called sponsors?" Bolan asked.

"No, he never mentioned names. Like I said, Bannon doesn't like to talk about them. He sees himself as a self-made man and all that, a warrior rising from the ashes of a crumbling civilization. I'm sure he doesn't like to think about his real roots, getting money from guys he claims to hate. But he's still taking money from his sponsors."

"That's where he got the jets." It was more a statement than a question.

"You got it. Built from scratch, in secret, with Bannon picking the fly-boys himself. I'm talking about some rich fat cats here. Billionaire oilmen, according to Bannon, some of them with political aspirations."

"And like I said, I'm getting mixed signals from a guy who was meant to be a sacrificial lamb," Bolan said.

"Look, I'm telling you what I know," Wilkins protested. "I've been by Bannon's side practically since day one, when he thought I could get my hands on some heavy hardware. The only reason I even know about these sponsors is because Bannon twice bragged about them, talking like he had them by the short hairs. That's his style."

Bolan had heard enough about the sponsors. Bannon came first. Only then, if he could pick up the trail of Bannon's source of big money, would he hunt down the fat cats playing the Right Hand of God's sick game from the sidelines and give them a taste of their main boy's poison.

"Tell me how Bannon plans to hit the White House."

"Full frontal assault. It's crazy, maybe even suicidal, I know. That's why I wanted out. I'm sure as hell not ready to give my life for some guy at war with the world."

"Sounds like you got smart," Bolan remarked. "What specifically do you know about Bannon's plan?"

"I told you, I was never privy to the full details."

"Don't jerk me around."

"Okay, okay. I think, but I'm not sure, Bannon is going to set off explosions at several major institutions across D.C. Exactly which institutions, I don't have a clue. His thinking, I guess, is that when every law-enforcement agency goes to inspect all the noise, Bannon intends to pull up right on Pennsylvania Avenue. Let me tell you, he's got enough men to pull it off. And he's got plenty more LAWs and other bazookas where that stash you took from him came from. Enough to put some gaping holes in the White House. He might even intend to blow down the front gates and storm the place, for all I know."

Bolan laid a dark look on Wilkins. "If I have something to say about it, he won't get that far."

"You better believe he's crazy enough to do exactly what he wants to do. So are the others. They don't care if they leave the White House grounds alive, they have that much hate and anger. Bannon sees himself ready to die for the cause, if that's what it takes. In his mind, it's all a statement about our times."

As his prisoner lapsed into a brooding silence, Bolan went over what he'd told Brognola about his strong hunch that the White House would come under attack. The big Fed had assured him that security would be beefed up, and that he would try to get the entire vicinity around the White House secured, cleared of all pedestrian traffic and tourists, although he wasn't sure he would get the President to go for it. However the Man decided to play it out, Bannon's sinister plot was taking solid shape: set off explosions around the city and while the police, FBI and other federal agents were moving in and securing what were intended to be diversionary targets, Bannon could make his grandstand statement.

Wilkins spoke again. "I know you were with the Indian and Denton at the compound. There's something you might want to know before we get back to town.''

The guy hesitated.

''What?''

Wilkins swallowed hard. ''Bannon had what he called a contingency plan, in case the law put the heat on him or things started to go sour. This afternoon, he sent out two teams. One snatched the Indian's daughter and the other team grabbed Denton's wife.''

''If something happens to Joe, Denton or their families, that vest of yours won't stop a bullet through your brain.''

Bolan kept Wilkins pinned with an icy stare before pushing the Blazer ahead with a burst of speed.

Time was up.

Judgment Day had arrived.

BOLAN FOUND Little Joe and Denton waiting for him when he pulled up in the motel lot. No sooner had he brought his Blazer to a stop, than the big man and ex-trooper were out of Denton's Jeep. As they made their way over, the murderous look the two men shot Wilkins warned Bolan it would be best to keep his prisoner close to him.

''I heard,'' Bolan told the two men.

Denton looked ready to cut loose with his AR-18 on Wilkins, but he turned his enraged stare on Bolan instead. "Now what? We get home to find our families have been kidnapped, notes pinned to our doors with knives telling us we better hand over what we took or they'll kill my wife and Joe's daughter."

"You did the smart thing by waiting for me," Bolan said.

"So you say," Denton growled, clearly on the verge of exploding. "I have to tell you, we'd almost decided to go after Bannon ourselves. What's this piece of shit doing here?"

"He's my prisoner," Bolan answered. "Maybe bait. Look, you need to keep yourselves under control and think clearly."

"Man, they do anything to Stan's wife or my daughter, and I'll die trying to kill every one of those bastards," Little Joe said, hefting the SPAS-12 to his chest. "They'll see hate like they've never known."

Suddenly lights turned on down the highway, snaring Bolan's attention. At least a dozen Jeeps and trucks, their high beams knifing through the blackness, began slowly rolling toward the motel. Pulling Wilkins close to him and unleathering his

Desert Eagle, Bolan waited, knowing already who was in that convoy of vehicles.

"Goddamn bastards!" Denton snarled, swinging his assault rifle toward the convoy.

"Don't do anything you might regret later," Bolan warned the two men. "Listen to me. If you want to keep your families alive, you'll let me play out Bannon's game."

A long moment later, he saw some of their rage lessen.

"We hear you," Denton finally answered.

They waited, lights washing over them as the vehicles fanned out, then stopped in the middle of the lot. Doors opened and dark figures, armed with shotguns or assault rifles, slowly walked into the lights. Standing their ground in the glare, with their breath pluming around them in the cold air, they looked like wraiths to Bolan. For several stretched seconds, none of the armed men moved. Then Bannon stepped forward until he stood a few yards short of Bolan's vehicle.

"Well, well," Bannon said, "look what we've got here. Three heroes and one traitor." He fixed his eyes on Wilkins. "I always knew you never had what it took to be one of us, Wilkins. But that's okay, because you'll be dead before the sun rises tomorrow. You've got my solemn promise on that." He then turned to Denton and Joe. "Now before you throw a little temper tantrum, your squaws are safe, at least for the moment. That brings us to you, Belasko. The man of the hour. Big hotshot Fed. Seeing that you've returned, I imagine I'm minus seven good men."

"You're minus seven men. In my mind, it isn't even debatable whether they were good."

Bannon stiffened, but kept his voice under control. "You know something, Belasko, I kind of liked you. I had some hopes for you."

"I'm pleased I could disappoint you, Bannon."

"How the hell can you stand there and talk to me like that? Whether you know it or not, you're one of us," Bannon said.

"That's where you're dead wrong. I'm not a damn thing like you, Bannon."

"It's a real shame you feel that way. I would give ten of my own for just one of you."

"You have—seven from the diner and the three you executed yourself. How many more lives are you willing to sacrifice?" Bolan said.

Hate burned in Bannon's eyes. "As many as it takes. Okay, hero, you drew the battle lines, so here it is. You've got ninety minutes to come into town with my merchandise and Wilkins. We make a trade, I give you back the two squaws. Everyone lives happily ever after.''

He smiled coldly. ''You think you're better than me, don't you, Belasko? Well, let me tell you, you're not going to beat me. I'm too damn good, too damn strong for you.''

There was a long moment of tight silence during which Bolan weighed up the odds that Bannon would give the order to his men to open fire. If that was the case, then the Executioner intended to put one through Bannon's eyes first. The man had to have known it, too, because as his men swung their weapons toward Bolan, the ex-FBI special agent waved a restraining hand.

''In case you're wondering, I've got Sheriff Maulin behind me on this one,'' Bannon went on. ''I have some dirt on the guy, regarding the supposed rape of a young girl up north a few years back. Maulin knows it's finished for him here. His bags are packed, and he's going all the way with me on this one. I'll let him think he's still useful and has a way out. But I own this town, Belasko. It's mine to do with what I want. I can burn down the whole goddamn place if I want to. No one's going to call Dawson. Everyone's too damn scared. They know that if I'm going down, so are they. Funny what fear can do to people." Bannon paused, then said, "If Dawson does show up, though, I've got enough rockets to spare a few on some state troopers. You're on your own, Belasko, you and your buddies. Remember, ninety minutes."

Bolan watched as the enemy slowly moved out of the lights and got into their vehicles. They backed out of the lot until the front of the motel was once again dark.

The Executioner went to his Blazer to get what he would need to go to war.

INSIDE HIS ROOM a few minutes later, Bolan was dressed in a blacksuit and outfitted with webbing, complete with pouches loaded with spare clips for the M-16, Beretta and Desert Eagle, grenades for the M-203 and shells for the Mossberg. After cracking a 30-round clip into the M-16 and loading the M-203 with a 40 mm round, Bolan turned to his allies. Wilkins sat slumped in a chair by the nightstand, looking utterly defeated.

"We're three men against not only Bannon and his goons, but it sounds like the whole town is rooting for that bastard," Denton said. "We also need to make sure that my wife and Joe's daughter are safe and unharmed when we go in there."

Bolan nodded. "That's the first thing. But let me handle the trade."

"You actually think Bannon is going to just hand over Annie and Rebecca?" Little Joe asked.

"He also wants Wilkins," Bolan stated, drawing a look of fear from the man in question.

"You Judas bastard!" Wilkins cried. "I helped you. Now you're going to hand me over, just like that? He'll put one through my brains on the spot."

"Not if I also offer to hand myself over," Bolan said.

"What do you mean?" Denton asked, baffled.

"I said I'll offer to hand myself over. I didn't say I'll become his prisoner," Bolan explained. "Bannon's going to need some insurance to make sure he gets out of town."

Denton's gaze narrowed with anxiety. "You're going to stall him, wait until we get our women back and out of the line of fire, then cut loose?"

"I'll let Bannon make that call."

"You're crazy, Belasko, but I like you," Little Joe said. "I'm beginning to think you care if Stan and me see Annie and Rebecca alive."

"There's nothing to think about, Joe. I do care. Or I'd just go in and hunt them down."

"Can I make a suggestion?" Little Joe asked. "Leave one of those rocket launchers with me and Stan. If it goes bad, you'll be right in the middle of it all. You'll need as many of them taken out as possible."

"I don't want it to go bad, Joe. I want your daughter and Denton's wife safely out of the way. When we go in there, it's going to be a test of wills between myself and Bannon. You make him panic, and he'll start shooting."

"What's to say that isn't his whole intent?" Denton asked.

Bolan didn't answer. He realized the man had a good point. They needed some leverage in case it did go bad. Okay, he'd hand over a few LAWs, then let Bannon make the call, but only after the two kidnapped women were set free. Then it would all depend on Bannon deciding whether a federal agent would make a better hostage than two innocent women.

Bolan nodded to Little Joe. "I'll show you how to operate the LAWs. Are we agreed, though, that I'll handle the situation when we get to town?"

He waited while Denton and Little Joe exchanged looks. Finally they gave the Executioner the nod.

Only Denton had something to add. "If it looks like it's going to go bad, if Bannon leaves us with no choice, then it's agreed we'll fight, side by side, and kill every last one of those scumbags."

"Let's just get your wife and Rebecca back," Bolan said.

Taking his prisoner by the arm, the soldier led his allies to the door and out into the night.

**11**

From the sheriff's second-story office in the Honor Courthouse, Bannon peered through the blind to survey the street below. With the exception of a few streetlights and the dull glow emanating from a couple of businesses, the town was dark and quiet. But it wasn't empty. Along the boardwalk, he spotted the shadowy armed figures of several of the local wannabes. He cursed their presence. They might prove a nuisance, and if they got in the way he intended to take them out. Just like he would Mike Belasko. Elsewhere, from positions of safety behind the gloomily lit windows of their offices, Bannon could make out the townspeople of Honor, the noncombatants eagerly waiting to watch the showdown. Sheep, Bannon thought disgustedly. It still amused him how so many of them had been cowed by fear. The entire town knew what had been going on for several years, that there was a paramilitary group in the mountains, right under their noses, pretty much doing what they wanted, when they wanted. Yet the townspeople had chosen to turn the other cheek. Bannon suspected there were reasons for their not taking a stand against him. They had either been hoping that he and his men would quietly pack up and leave or be dealt with by the so-called law, allowing them to keep their lily-white hands free of blood. No, they hadn't dared to speak out against him or his legion, hadn't even gone to the state police. They just wanted to be left alone to go about the drudgery of their foolish lives, Bannon reflected, feeling renewed contempt for the town. A town called Honor, he decided, deserved the worst, if only because there wasn't a shred of honor to be found in the whole county. There was only the Right Hand of God.

Bannon continued to assess the situation, while feeling the eyes of his men, the sheriff, his deputies and the two women boring into the back of his head. In front of the frontiersman statue, he had a dozen vehicles strung out in a phalanx. When the shooting started, and he knew it would because he wanted to kill Belasko like no man he had ever wanted to kill, he and his men would use the vehicles as cover. If some of those vehicles were disabled by gunfire, there were more Jeeps and trucks just outside of town, ready to evacuate them when this little showdown with the Fed was finished. Apart from the crate of LAWs and three Armbrust bazookas he had on hand, he had another fifteen rocket launchers and one hundred pounds of C-4 plastique stashed nearby. An hour earlier, he had touched base with his followers from Kansas. They were already airborne, and he'd let them know that the evacuation site had been changed from the state line to an empty field twenty miles outside of town.

The more Bannon thought about Belasko, the more his blood burned with hate. The big Fed had taken sides against him, had killed seven of his soldiers and was now dangling a traitor over his head like a worm on a hook. Worse, Belasko had put an edge of fear in him, banged a nail of doubt in his mind that maybe he wasn't invincible—that he could somehow fail. Nobody did that to a man who was to spearhead a revolution. Didn't Belasko know that Bannon's crusade would set the country back on its natural course before it was messed up by the Civil Rights Movement? Didn't that man understand that the government he worked for was the real enemy, the true oppressor of any people left in

America who were worth a damn? Well, Bannon thought, if he couldn't change a man's thinking, the only thing left to do was get him out of the way. Permanently.

He turned away from the window and faced his soldiers. They were mostly grim-faced, all armed and ready to fight. They would not be going out in a blaze of glory, especially not in this hillbilly town. Bannon fully intended to survive the night with whatever it took, and so did his men. It reassured him that they looked as hard as steel, their stares as cold as the icy touch of death. It was only Maulin who seemed to be having a bad case of the nerves.

The sheriff sat hunched over his desk, his ashtray heaped with a dozen butts from chain-smoking. For the third time in fifteen minutes, Bannon saw him reach for his pint of whiskey. After a deep swig, Maulin wiped some sweat off his brow. His two deputies, Stone and Michaels, stood behind the man. Both clean-cut men were young and hard, honorary members of the movement, given to Maulin by Bannon after his election. The deputies were good men in Bannon's mind. They kept the sheriff on a tight leash when he had second thoughts about hiding or covering for a heavily armed force of God's chosen soldiers.

As Bannon looked at the sweating, fidgeting sheriff, he had the urge to walk over to him and slap some sense into him. The way the sheriff was throwing the evil eye around the room, anyone would think he was an innocent man. Well, Bannon knew that was far from being the case. When Bannon had been looking for a suitable spot in the Rockies' wilderness, he had been informed of Maulin's strange sexual tastes by one of his ex-cop soldiers. There had been a setup, some pictures taken and Bannon had put his proposal to Maulin. Bannon had helped him become sheriff with some payoffs to the right people.

So, after being elected, all Maulin had to do was to keep his mouth shut, his eyes and ears open for any troublemakers or his nose tuned to the scent that the state police or Feds were snooping around for gun-toting rabble-rousers in the mountains. But that was ancient history, before the killing of a state trooper and the arrival of the big Fed. Bannon couldn't see where Maulin was doing him much good anymore.

The sheriff checked his watch again. "Where is he? It's already been ninety minutes, Bannon."

"He'll be here."

"This goddamn waiting's getting me down."

"Have another drink, Sheriff. It's about all you're good for right now," Bannon said.

"It's so easy for you, isn't it?" Maulin said. "You can take off when this is over, go carry on with your crusade. Me, I'm finished in this town. I'll spend the rest of my life hiding or looking over my shoulder."

Bannon ignored him, leering instead at the two women. They sat in wooden chairs, surrounded by several of his men. He was somewhat impressed at how composed they seemed. They were tough, solid and damn good-looking women, he had to give them that. For just a second he felt a stab of jealous anger, wondering what it would be like to get either of them in the sack. He eyed their high, sculpted cheekbones, their dark fiery eyes and silky raven-black hair. They were firm, tight and well-rounded in all the right places. Bannon felt his blood getting fired with lust and told himself to get it under control.

"This crazy stunt you pulled," Maulin whined. "All you did was make me an accessory to kidnapping."

"Stop your blubbering, Maulin. I already told you you've got a free ride out with us. What more do you want?"

"Reassurance that Dawson won't just pop up, for starters. What are you going to do then? Start killing cops?"

"Let's hope for his sake that it doesn't come to that," Bannon said. "Let's also hope it doesn't come to you bailing out on me when this is over. Don't forget, I've got some pictures a few people around here might be interested in seeing."

"You start shooting this town up, the state police will be here before you know it," Maulin said.

Bannon felt his blood pressure shoot straight into his ears. "Let me tell you something, Sheriff. There's not a man in this county with enough balls to stand up to me. What I see when I look around are a bunch of people too damn scared to do anything other than be afraid that their little worlds might be shattered. Yet no one has ever stood up to me or my men. Sure, they may come to you and do a little whining, but that's as far as it's ever gone. What you see here is what's going

on across the country—people cowed with fear
and silence, afraid to speak the truth because
they think they've lost the upper hand, so what's
the use in bothering. Doesn't it make you sick,
Maulin? Don't you want your balls back? I do.
That's why I'm not worried about any state police. I'm unstoppable, I'm unbeatable. I believe
in what I'm doing. I'm prepared to go all the
way, give up my life, if I have to, even for this
country that used to be great but now needs
someone like me to kick it in the ass.''

Maulin stared at Bannon as if seeing him for
the first time. ''You're insane,'' he said.

''I'm a realist. And I'm determined. What I
am is what everyone in this town would like to
be. And that's a warrior with a just and right-
eous cause.''

Suddenly Denton's wife made a little sound,
and Bannon turned to look at her. It was as if she
were judging him, Bannon thought, peering right
through him with those dark eyes of hers. How
defiant would she be, Bannon wondered, if he
stripped her right there and bent her over Maulin's desk?

''Did I say something funny?'' Bannon asked.

''Nothing about any of this is funny,'' Annie
Thundersong said. ''Actually it is all very sad.''

"You act like you think you know something I don't. Maybe you want to share your secret with me."

Thundersong shrugged. "There is no secret where a man like you is concerned. You are like some virus that can only stay strong by infecting others or feeding off their fear. All you really hate and fear, Bannon, is yourself. You are only as happy as the amount of suffering and pain you can cause others."

Bannon was aware his men were watching him, waiting to see how he would respond to this affront. "You don't think I can take this town apart, just walk away and leave it in ruins, do you?"

Thundersong stayed solid. "I think you are going to do whatever it is you are going to do."

Bannon laughed, but he knew there was some uncertainty in the sound. "You've got spunk, lady. Denton did all right."

"Thank you. I wish I could say the same for you."

He took a step toward the woman, who braced herself for a blow, but the sound of engines rumbling outside, followed by the glow of lights hitting the blinds, stopped him. Bannon and several of his men went to the window.

He spotted the two vehicles he had been waiting for slowly roll down the street. Midway down, he saw Denton's Jeep stop while the Blazer went on. Some distance from the defensive line formed by Bannon's vehicles, the Blazer swung sideways on, then stopped, and the big Fed stepped out. Bannon saw that he had an assault rifle slung across one shoulder with what appeared to be an attached grenade launcher. So, the man had come prepared to fight. Bannon had to give him credit for knowing the deal.

"So he's come to do battle with the bad guys," Peterson commented.

"Let's go find out just how bad *he* is," Bannon said.

LEAVING WILKINS in the Blazer, Bolan hauled Bannon's crate out of the back of the vehicle, then dumped it in the middle of the street. Denton and Little Joe flanked Denton's Jeep, their weapons poised. The LAW was still inside the vehicle, tube extended and its missile ready to be launched. Bolan hoped the two men wouldn't need to use their weapons, having told them before they'd left the motel to say and do nothing, but he feared that a peaceful conclusion to this exchange with Bannon was a false hope. It was going to turn ugly, and he could feel it in the cold mountain air all around him. If he was going to get Denton's wife and Joe's daughter back, there was no other way but to confront Bannon. It would be a test of wills, Bolan knew, and he could only offer himself in place of the two women and hope Bannon would take the bait.

The soldier went to get Wilkins out of the Blazer. "Don't do anything stupid, and you might live through this night," he warned the man. "Try to run and you'll know what real pain is."

Bolan unslung his M-16. As he took in his surroundings, he realized just how much he didn't like the setup. To his left flank, shrouded in the shadows of the boardwalk, Bolan spotted some of the men he had fought the night before. Most of them sported bandages, and all of them toted assault rifles. Altogether, he counted seven locals, but he was aware there were probably more armed men scattered throughout the hidden corners of town.

His eyes swept the buildings on both sides of the street. He could detect maybe two dozen people clustered behind the doors and windows. Whether they were spectators or possible combatants he couldn't be sure. But unless they tried to get in his way or hinder his fight, he hoped he could safely ignore them.

Bolan turned his full attention onto the courthouse. Only one light showed in the building. Moments earlier, he'd seen the silhouettes of men against the window blind, but then they'd disappeared.

There was nothing to do but wait and be vigilant.

The Executioner didn't have to wait long.

The big double doors to the courthouse opened to disgorge Bannon and his horde, their hard-soled shoes ringing as they marched down the courthouse steps then through the town square.

Bolan gave Wilkins a quick check. The guy looked terrified. As well he might, because all Wilkins meant to Bolan was a promise to Bannon he wasn't going to keep.

Feeling the tension in the air like some oppressive weight, the Executioner watched as the enemy slipped between the parked vehicles. They kept their weapons canted to their shoulders or cupped in their hands. As they closed in, Bolan could almost smell the insane hunger of bad men who wanted nothing but to wreak death and destruction.

Bolan spotted Bannon, who was cradling a futuristic-looking Austrian Steyr assault rifle. To have gotten his hands on international firepower like that, Bolan knew the ex-Fed had to be well connected. It made him wonder just who, and how many, in higher places had given their souls to Bannon's twisted cause, how far the tentacles of the Right Hand of God stretched.

The guy Bolan had learned was called Peterson had the women in his clutches. He and his charges followed Bannon as he stepped away from the others, stopping about a dozen yards from Bolan. The soldier scrutinized the two women and was thankful to see they appeared unharmed.

"Are both of you all right?" he asked.

They nodded.

Aside from being every bit as beautiful as he'd known they would be, Bolan discerned the certain tough quality in their eyes that told him they were fighters, not ones to be bullied into submission by the likes of Bannon.

"Just like I said it would be, isn't it, Belasko?" Bannon suddenly called out. "You and me." He made a production of breathing in the air. "Can't you just smell the fear? Kind of invigorating, wouldn't you say? Let me ask you something, Belasko. You think any of these people deserve to go on living?''

As Bannon's voice cut through the night, Bolan's narrowed gaze wandered over the pack. Bringing up the rear, while sticking close to the parked cars, were Sheriff Maulin and two men in identical brown uniforms, sheepskin coats and Stetson hats. Bolan assumed they were Maulin's deputies. Still more cops gone bad.

Abruptly one of the armed shadows barked, ''When you're done with the bastard, Bannon, how about giving us a few pieces of what's left?''

''Shut your mouths!'' Bannon roared.

Without warning, the ex-FBI man thrust the muzzle of his Steyr into the ear of one of the women. She closed her eyes but didn't flinch or buckle. She had obviously prepared herself for this moment, had resolved not to beg for her life.

Bolan swung his M-16 on Bannon. ''Don't do it!'' he warned. In response, two dozen shotguns and assault rifles drew target acquisition on him. ''Let them go. You can take me in their place.''

Bannon laughed. ''Really? Well, in that case . . .''

Bolan felt his finger tighten on the M-16's trigger as the ugly smile stayed frozen on the hate-monger's face.

Bannon lowered the assault rifle to his side, then nodded to Peterson. "Let the Indian's daughter go."

Peterson released Little Joe's daughter, who held her ground for a long and dangerous moment, staring at Denton's wife as if silently telling her she didn't want to leave without her. Damn, but the kid had guts, Bolan thought, silently urging her to flee. Finally the young woman moved away from Peterson.

"Keep moving," Bolan told her, tight-lipped, as she drew level with him. He kept his sights locked on to Bannon.

She moved on. Moments later, he heard the brief exchange between Little Joe and his daughter, the big man telling her to get into the Jeep and stay there. A stretched second later the Executioner caught the sound of the Jeep's door closing hard. One innocent out of the way. One to go.

"Okay, hero. Now, how about my crate?" Bannon said.

"Come and get it. My offer still stands. Wilkins and me for Denton's wife."

Bannon turned to the armed locals. "If you want to make yourselves useful, get that crate and bring it to me," he snapped.

The implication of Bannon's order didn't escape Bolan. The guy was bringing new players into the picture. He suspected their use would go beyond retrieving the rockets.

Obviously the locals were leery, too, and none of them moved.

"Now!" Bannon roared.

With that, the shadows started toward the crate. Bolan could feel their stares drilling into him. But they were following Bannon's orders, acting as his lackeys. The warrior stayed ready to cut down the armed man if they so much as lifted a weapon in his direction. The guy Bolan had dubbed Red, who had lost big money to Little Joe in eight ball and taken his own knife through his leg, limped toward Bannon, covering the Executioner with his shotgun while the others hauled the crate.

"Open it," Bannon ordered.

They did. Bolan prepared to core a round through Bannon's forehead if he discovered one of the LAWs was missing.

But the moment of danger passed, as Bannon glanced down into the crate, apparently satisfied. The locals took the crate to one of the vehicles. "All right, Belasko, now give me Wilkins."

"Let Denton's wife go first."

Bannon's expression hardened, and he motioned to the locals to draw up. Bolan tensed, suspecting that the enemy leader was about to thrust a new dimension into his plan. As the locals closed in, Bolan heard Bannon say, "You want to be one of us, here's your chance." He then grabbed the big redheaded guy and pulled him close. "The only way in life is to stand tall in the trenches, to dig in and face it down. Do you want to stand hard and show me what you've got?"

Smith nodded, turning a hate-filled stare on Bolan.

"Are you prepared to give your life for the movement?" Bannon rasped into Smith's ear while keeping his gaze riveted on Bolan. "Answer me!"

Smith nodded again. Bolan hadn't caught Bannon's words, but he was sure that the guy had just become a sacrificial lamb.

Bannon smiled strangely. "Okay, Belasko, I'll turn Denton's wife loose. You say you want to give yourself up to me, but I don't see you putting down your weapons.''

"Let her go first."

"I've got your word of honor as a man?"

"Let the woman go, Bannon."

"You don't trust me?"

Bolan was a heartbeat away from squeezing the trigger, drawing a bead right between Bannon's eyes. "As soon as she's out of the way. If she doesn't make it, you won't either. You may kill me, you may not. But I can guarantee that I sure as hell will put one right between your eyes first."

There was a heartbeat where it was all poised to go bad. The only sound Bolan caught was the hard breathing of a terror-stricken Wilkins.

"Let Denton's squaw go," Bannon snapped to Peterson.

Bolan didn't like it. Something in the man's look and voice warned the Executioner the moment was ready to explode.

Peterson shoved Thundersong toward Bolan.

"Put it down, Belasko," Bannon growled, inching closer toward Smith, but Bolan didn't budge. "You're starting to really piss me off. I told you to drop the weapon and get yourself and Wilkins over here.''

"We'll proceed when the woman's out of the way."

"Now! Drop your damn weapon!"

Bolan slid toward Thundersong, knowing the moment of danger was right at the edge. "Get behind me," he ordered.

The woman slipped behind him.

Rage turned Bannon's eyes into two bulging white orbs. "You think you can mess with me! Is that what you think?"

It happened just as Bolan had expected. Knowing it was coming, and moving like a flash of lightning, the Executioner grabbed Thundersong, shielding her as he flung her behind the Blazer a heartbeat before Bannon snatched Smith and cut loose with his Steyr.

Only Bannon's target was Wilkins, who took the full brunt of his leader's volley in the chest.

Left with no choice but to fight with all the fury and speed he could muster, Bolan sprayed the line of hardmen, then dived for cover when Bannon's soldiers unleashed a furious barrage in return.

Then, out of the corner of his eye, Bolan caught a flaming missile streaking past his position.

The LAW rocket turned night into day as it impacted, with hellish thunder, dead center of the line of vehicles.

**12**

Countless times Bolan had risked his life in the line of fire against great and often seemingly insurmountable odds, but always with the intention of surviving to carry on the good fight.

Bolan believed that there were still good people in the world, worth fighting, saving and even dying for, if that's what it took. These thoughts flashed through Bolan's mind as he faced down Bannon and his horde. The war of Honor was brutally and suddenly under way.

The firestorm the enemy unleashed thudded into the Blazer, pinning Bolan down momentarily. With glass splintering over his head and slugs whining and sparking off the asphalt, the soldier knew he had only seconds to act before a stray round tore into either himself or Thundersong, or sizzling lead ignited the fuel tank. A quick glance over his shoulder told him that Denton and Little Joe were pounding away with their weapons, a combined barrage from the assault rifle and the SPAS-12 tearing into the enemy's position.

Bolan took Thundersong by the arm. "Stay behind me. When I tell you to run, hit the walk, stay low and get out of town. Don't go for your husband, just run!"

Shielding the woman behind him, the soldier swiftly headed for the back of the Blazer, the enemy fire concentrated on the front of the vehicle. Bolan drew a deep breath. "Now!"

The Executioner whirled toward the front of the vehicle, cutting loose with his M-16, doing his best to take out anyone who sought cover behind the flaming wreckage. In his line of battle vision, he could see bodies strewed in front of the phalanx of cars, some of them still moving around or crying out in pain. But it was the guys who were able to dart for cover in the deepest shadows of the vehicles that Bolan went for. Bolan couldn't be certain whether he'd taken out Bannon with his initial burst. One guy with a bandaged leg was stretched out in a pool of blood, and Bolan could hear him calling out for God's mercy.

On this night there would be no mercy, no redemption for the enemy, no salvation for the town of Honor.

Hideous screams knifed the air, as Bolan dropped three targets with a long sweeping burst, then he added a 40-mm strike into the heart of the enemy. Triggering the M-203, Bolan streaked for the walk and the cover provided by the other parked vehicles.

Adding to the murderous chaos and confusion, the high-explosive grenade ripped apart three more vehicles, the ear-shattering blast hurling twisted wreckage and body parts in all directions. But just as before, the Right Hand of God came back at the Executioner, tracking him with a fury that once more revealed just how determined they were in their perverse cause.

A hurricane of bullets washed over Bolan's cover a beat before he reached temporary safety behind a pickup truck. He fired at shadows dancing beyond the flames, then saw a hardman spin and drop.

Bolan checked on Thundersong and found her doing exactly what he'd told her to—running hard and low down the boardwalk.

But then Bolan discovered that Denton was not satisfied to stay put and provide additional cover for his wife. He was angling sideways from the Jeep, unleashing his AR-18 bombardment on the enemy, while bellowing for his wife to get down. A tracking line of bullets began to stitch the street around Denton.

Quickly Bolan reloaded his M-203, sending another explosive message of doom into the heart of the Right Hand of God. The blast silenced the enemy guns for a few critical moments while he primed the grenade launcher. Ramming a fresh 30-round magazine into the M-16, he popped up to spray the line of vehicles, sending hardmen scurrying for cover as his firestorm raked them. It was just enough to allow Denton to get to his wife and grab her by the arm, propelling her down the street.

Just as the warrior had expended the last 5.56-mm round to keep the enemy's attention focused on himself, he caught sight of a tall shadow darting to the side of the fire. In the glow of the flames Bolan saw the sharp features of Bannon. Something metallic glinted in the man's hands, and it took only a split second for Bolan to recognize it as the MM-1 Multiround projectile launcher.

"Get out of here!" Bolan roared at Little Joe, who was still holding his turf by thundering away with the SPAS-12.

The soldier pumped one more grenade into the line of vehicles. Suddenly there was a chugging sound, but Bolan was already moving for deeper cover. He flung himself through a doorway, plunging into the blackness of the building an instant before the truck he'd used as cover was blown apart and kicked across the boardwalk. The chassis connected with the canopy stretched over the boardwalk, and brought it crashing down in an avalanche of fire and jagged shards, before the flaming heap slammed through the front wall of the building. The Executioner ran for his life, down a hallway toward the back door he could see located at the farthest end of the place. He dived headlong through the back door just as the next series of thunderous explosions crashed behind him, sending out a screaming ball of fire.

A BLINDING FLASH OF RAGE had overwhelmed Bannon when he knew beyond a shadow of a doubt that Belasko had stood up to him. The big Fed had held his ground and gotten what he wanted, and for that alone Bannon had to grudgingly give him some respect. At the instant it had all exploded, and the three of them—Wilkins, Belasko and the woman—had all become a jumble of faceless entities in his murderous vision: Belasko grabbing the woman, then diving out of the line of fire, Wilkins standing frozen in front of the Blazer, soldiers awaiting his order to open fire. Consumed with a hate to do nothing but kill, Bannon had fixed his rage on the only standing available target—Wilkins.

Then all hell had broken loose. As the first explosion ripped through his defensive line, Bannon realized that Belasko had outsmarted him. He'd held back one of the LAWs and the Indian was using it to shave the odds.

But Bannon was far from finished with the three of them, or the town, for that matter. As soon as his human shield was hit by Belasko's initial burst, Bannon had scrambled for cover. Luckily the blast had struck on the far right flank of the vehicles, sparing the bulk of his men. During the first few moments of panic, he had gone to work quickly to reclaim the initiative and so had his soldiers.

When a second and then a third explosion had rocked the night and left Bannon untouched, he figured God was surely on his side.

Even after three deadly fireballs had been inflicted on his men by his adversaries, Bannon found he still had plenty of savagely determined guns pouring it back on the trio. But he had expected nothing less all along from his troops. As he had searched the killing ground ahead through the flames and swirling smoke, Bannon had caught sight of Thundersong reaching the arms of her husband. Once again, the bile of failure had threatened to worm its way into his throat. That's when he'd decided to get serious. He pulled the MM-1 from its crate, relieved that the stash he'd gotten back from Belasko was undamaged by the explosions and any flying wreckage. Four LAWs at his disposal should be enough to bring down Honor and allow him and his men to escape the situation.

Moving behind the wall of flames and smoke, avoiding the bullets from Belasko and his allies, Bannon armed the MM-1, then pulverized his enemy's cover with a 38-mm strike that hurled the vehicle through the building. Moments earlier, he'd seen Belasko bulldozing through the doorway of the hardware store. The store was full of all kinds of chemicals. It was perfect. Not only would he kill the man, but he would set off a firestorm that would ravage the entire town.

Teeth clenched in an expression of fury, Bannon pumped three high-explosive rounds into the hardware store. The ensuing ball of fire that vaporized the building before erupting into blinding mushroom clouds mesmerized Bannon for a long moment. It was a beautiful, awe-inspiring sight, all that blazing glory shooting for the sky, blinding and raging fingers of fire hurtling debris everywhere, the sound of searing flames filling his ears like music. Nothing could survive that blast.

Following the earthshaking blasts, Bannon found panic had gripped the townspeople. He saw them burst from their homes and head for their vehicles, while some took off on foot. Bannon was surprised at how calm he felt. Honor would burn to the ground. Even if someone called the fire department, or alerted the state police, it would do no good. This was his night.

With the MM-1 held low by his side, Bannon quickly inspected his trucks and Jeeps. He found five undamaged vehicles, including the truck that housed the bulk of his rocket firepower. He began to bark out orders. He told Peterson and ten others to get the intact vehicles out of town and to wait for him. He ordered six men to form two three-man teams, to split up and check behind the building he'd destroyed, which was now engulfed in flames, and to kill anything that moved.

As they went to carry out his orders, Bannon turned his sights on the dead and the dying. At first glance it looked like at least eight of his men had died during the opening strike. One of them had been hurled against the frontiersman statue and lay in a twisted heap near the courthouse steps. The impact of his body had broken part of the statue, leaving jagged teeth of stone at the base.

"Goddammit, Bannon, I told you... Didn't I... warn you..."

Maulin. Bannon found the sheriff lying in a pool of blood, a hand clamped over his shoulder. The sheriff's two deputies had also survived, but not unharmed, and they lay stretched out in the street, moaning and nursing bloody limbs. Bannon didn't have time for wounded men.

As engines began to roar to life and vehicles started to pull out, he unholstered a Detonics pistol from beneath his coat and pumped two .45ACP rounds through the sheriff's face. He then turned to the deputies and gave them the same .45 facial. It was too bad, he thought. The deputies were fine young men, but excess baggage would hinder him. Plus they knew too much.

Before the sound of the shots had completely faded from his ears, Bannon became aware of flashing lights just beyond the town proper.

The state police were arriving.

Anticipating the prospect of doing battle with the real law, Bannon moved away from the carnage and the crackling tongues of fire. He watched cars and trucks roaring down the street in reverse, the drivers in a panic to get out of town. He picked out his human shield, Smith, crawling from the kill zone, and cored a .45 slug through the back of his head. He had counted six squad cars racing into the mouth of the town before he noticed that Peterson and the vehicles slated for evacuation had stopped.

"Hold up," Bannon yelled at Peterson. "Any man not driving, fall out and flank me. When we clear the way, Peterson, we'll all go together."

Soldiers disgorged from the vehicles, slamming fresh clips into their assault rifles. Bannon yelled at two soldiers to grab a LAW from the crate behind him and fall in.

Then Bannon discovered that Wilkins wasn't dead.

Off to his side, Wilkins was struggling to sit up against the Blazer. His coat and shirt were in shreds, but there was no blood. Wilkins was wearing Kevlar.

Angling toward the traitor, Bannon cocked a cold grin at him, drew his Detonics and shot the man twice in the head.

Feeling touched by divine magic, Bannon tucked away the Detonics, hefted the MM-1 and walked toward the state police.

STAN DENTON AND HIS WIFE ran until they were near the edge of town. When he turned to look back, Denton saw Little Joe racing his vehicle out of town, his daughter beside him in the front seat.

Then Denton heard the tremendous explosions. He stared at the spot where he'd seen Belasko disappear. Pain and regret choked his throat, but he didn't want to believe that the man who had saved the lives of his wife and Little Joe's daughter was dead.

Denton slapped a fresh 30-round magazine into his weapon and chambered the first round.

"Stay here," he told his wife.

Thundersong grabbed Denton's arm. "No, don't go. They'll kill you. There's nothing more you can do."

Grim determination steeled Denton's eyes even as he softened his voice for his wife's sake. "Stay here and wait for me. I'll be back."

"If the man was caught in that explosion, he is dead."

"We don't know that. If he's alive, he'll need my help."

There was a moment when Denton thought his wife would protest further, but she released her hold on him and nodded. There was a soft light of respect in Thundersong's eyes, and Denton could read the gratitude on his wife's face for the man who had come to face down Bannon. Even though Thundersong feared the worst, Denton knew she understood.

What Denton also hoped she understood was that he had to see Bannon and the others dead, or none of them would ever again know a moment's peace.

After waiting for his wife to retreat deeper into the shadows, he moved out. He caught sight of Little Joe bounding onto the boardwalk across the street, having abandoned the Jeep. The big man had his SPAS-12, ready to mow down anything that came his way. Denton saw Little Joe give him the thumbs-up. He knew Little Joe so well that he could almost hear the words he'd known the man to use several times before when his back was to the wall.

*It's a good day to die.*

When Denton saw the shadows of Bannon and his men walk out of the raging fire at the end of town, he suspected he and Little Joe might do just that. But he owed Mike Belasko. Or, at the very least, he owed the memory of the man who had saved Thundersong and Little Joe's daughter.

**13**

While Bannon was scrambling to seize back the night, Mack Bolan was picking himself off the ground in the back alley. Having hurtled through the back door like a human missile, with shrieking balls of fire racing after him, it took him long and critical moments to gather himself, and another few seconds for the ringing to fade just enough in his ears for him to catch the volley of automatic-weapons' fire in the street beyond.

Ramming a fresh magazine into his M-16, the soldier moved out in the direction of the courthouse.

By the corner of the building, Bolan hit a combat crouch. He spotted Bannon, and was about to draw target acquisition on the Right Hand of God's leader when staccato bursts of automatic weapons rang out, forcing him to hug the edge of the building. His sights having been fixed on Bannon, Bolan had almost missed the hardmen, either behind their leader or near the far right flank of the devastated vehicles. For agonizing minutes, Bolan was pinned down by merciless autofire.

WITH A FRESH 9-shot magazine in his SPAS-12, Little Joe was ready to do what he had been wanting to do for more than three years. The time had come for him and Denton to dish back some of what they'd had to put up with. As far as Little Joe was concerned, no one in Honor was innocent. Perhaps some of the townspeople hadn't abused him directly, but he had seen their faces, caught their whispered consent to those who had bullied and even beaten him, and threatened his daughter or Denton's wife. A man could only choke down so much before he exploded. Little Joe knew that he wouldn't gun down an unarmed Honor citizen, but if they were cut down by Bannon or his gunmen, then so be it. A man was either good or bad, he had always believed, and during the course of a man's life he had to choose a side. To not take one side or the other was anathema to Little Joe. He could hold some respect for bad men because they at worst made a stand for themselves and had principles, such as they were. To stay in the limbo of in-between good and bad made a man less than nothing in his eyes. That was what most of the people of Honor were to him. Nothing. This night they had been jolted out of their limbo.

After giving his friend on the other side of the street the thumbs-up, the big man moved down the walk with all the real or imagined determination of his Cherokee ancestors heading out to do battle. What had mattered most, the safety of his daughter and Denton's wife, was behind them. All that was left to do was to kill the enemy or die a warrior. Since the death of his wife by cancer five years earlier, Little Joe figured he'd been dying a slow death every day, seeking oblivion through the bottle, the gambling and the confrontations with locals who simply hated him for being what he was. To die a warrior would be an honorable thing.

Mike Belasko had proved himself a friend and a warrior. The thought that the man who had put his life on the front line to get his daughter and Thundersong back might have perished in the explosion knifed through Little Joe's heart. But it served as fuel for his fire.

Ahead of him, he saw the soldiers of hate walk out of the flames, armed to the teeth.

Behind him, the law raced into the mouth of the town.

Little Joe also saw the fine citizens of Honor scattering like frightened sheep, fleeing burning buildings or leaping into their vehicles. The spectators had become potential targets for Bannon's hate and rage, or human shields, depending on what the man would need. In their panic, many of the citizens had crashed their cars and trucks into each other, while others had decided flight by foot was more prudent. Women were wailing up and down the street, while some of the men viciously cursed the destruction of their town. With all the chaos swirling out in the street, Little Joe had to wait to pick out his targets.

He didn't have to wait long for the next stage of the battle to erupt.

Across the street, from behind a parked Chevy pickup, he could see Denton was cutting loose with his assault rifle, his bullets drilling into one of Bannon's men.

Just as Bannon and two of his soldiers unleashed their rocket barrage on the state police, who had reached the battle zone, Little Joe began pounding away with his SPAS-12. One of the hardmen took the full brunt of 12-gauge death in the stomach, the blast flinging him through the windshield of a vintage Thunderbird.

Soon the enemy became aware of Little Joe's presence on the boardwalk, but the big man kept sweeping thundering death over the street. Then, out of the corner of his eye, he saw a few of Bannon's gunmen launch an all-out bombardment with their weapons on someone at the corner of the post office. A grin split Little Joe's face.

Belasko was alive.

In the next moment, just as he blasted out the windshield of one of Bannon's escape vehicles, fire raced through every nerve ending of Little Joe's body and he found himself plummeting through a plate-glass window.

FOR NO APPARENT REASON, two of the hardmen who had been raking Bolan's cover with blazing lead fury were suddenly kicked into the street. Chancing a peek around the corner of the building, Bolan discovered why.

Like some giant avenging angel, Little Joe came rolling down the walk. From the light of the fires, Bolan could see that the big man's poncho was drenched in blood.

Through the relentless stammer of weapons' fire, Bolan stayed low as he raced for the cover of flaming wreckage dead ahead. Firing on the run, the warrior downed two hardmen, then forged into the noxious black clouds of smoke. With his second-last 40-mm grenade loaded into the M-203, Bolan was hellbent on thwarting Bannon's flight from town.

But the enemy carried on with its savage intent to flee.

A delayed blast from nearby wreckage threw Bolan off the hunt for a moment, and he hit the dirt as debris banged off the ground beside him. Hauling himself onto his knee, Bolan locked his sights on one of the vehicles that the enemy soldiers were boarding.

With the shriek of rubber grabbing asphalt drilling his ears, Bolan gave the enemy's vehicle some lead then triggered the M-203. The missile impacted downrange. Whether the vehicle held Bannon, Bolan didn't know, but he at least cut the numbers some more as the Jeep was obliterated inside a roiling ball of fire.

Swiftly moving away from the scorching bands of fire around him, the Executioner gave the town a hard search. In the distance, on his left flank, he made out a shadow blazing away at the rampaging vehicles with an assault rifle. Edging down the street, senses alert, Bolan recognized the shadow as Denton.

Sustained fire from the AR-18 and the SPAS-12 washed over another of Bannon's vehicles. There was a sudden burst of flames as the fuel tank ignited, then the vehicle hammered up the walk and crashed through a building. Fire instantly leaped to life, and more shadowy figures scurried for parked vehicles.

As Bolan moved down the street, a bloody figure rose, weapon raised. The warrior stitched the man with a quick burst and walked on, the fires of Honor filling his eyes.

**14**

Had he not been so pumped up with adrenaline and still brutally aware that the fight was far from over, Mack Bolan would have been stunned by the carnage around him.

Dead men, glass and jagged smoking debris were strewed everywhere. Huge clouds of black smoke billowed into the sky as both sides of the town were eaten up by the raging firestorm. Men and women were scrambling over what was left of their town, or holding and consoling loved ones or friends. Some of them stared at him with looks ranging from fear to pure hate and accusation while others cursed out loud.

Little Joe limped up behind Bolan, who gave the big man a concerned look.

He wore his familiar grin, but he winced, his face a bloody mask of cuts and scratches. "It went clean through my shoulder," he told Bolan. "I also took one through the leg, and it sure didn't help my handsome mug that I took a swan dive through a window, but I'll live.''

Grateful above all else that his allies and their families had made it, Bolan nodded, as Denton, Thundersong and Little Joe's daughter converged on them.

Again Bolan searched the ruins littering the street and the roaring mountains of fire, but he found nothing other than the dead or the wounded. Bannon's destruction of Honor looked complete. Then he heard several groans coming from around and beyond the fiery graveyard of cruisers. Investigating closer, he came upon the mutilated bodies of at least five troopers, as well as Captain Dawson and another lawman, who lay in pools of blood. They had both taken either bullets or shrapnel, and both of them were clinging to life.

Bolan moved to Dawson first, and crouched by the lawman.

The captain struggled to focus his eyes on Bolan. ''You were right, Belasko. You knew it would go down like this.''

Being right was small consolation. The lives of two lawmen were hanging in the balance, and they needed immediate medical attention.

"I've got a radio in my Jeep, Captain," Denton said, joining Bolan. The other three came up behind him.

"You know the routine," Dawson said.

"Get some medical help here first," Bolan advised Denton.

"Right, then I'll get every unit in this state after Bannon."

"Did you see him get away?" Bolan asked Denton.

"I took out the windshield of his vehicle, but then I saw the bastard pop up. I saw him grinning back at me."

"Are there any fields or open stretches near here that could land aircrafts?" Bolan asked.

"Only one I know of in these parts," Denton replied.

"Make that call, then tell me exactly where it is. I'll need your vehicle, Denton."

"I'm going with you."

Bolan caught Thundersong looking at her husband pleadingly. "No," he said. "You've done enough. You're needed here more."

Denton looked set to protest, but finally he nodded and moved off to his Jeep.

Thundersong spoke. "I don't know who you are or why you came here, or even why you risked your life to save us, but I thank you. We all thank you. We won't forget you.''

"It's enough that you're all alive," Bolan told her.

Dawson groaned again. "Belasko, get the hell out of here and go nail those bastards. I'll tell Denton to alert my men to what you're doing. I'm putting you in charge. You hear me?"

Bolan's eyes locked with Dawson's pain-filled gaze, and he nodded.

Knowing that Bannon was en route to his fleet of jets, the soldier made his way back to the other end of town. He was down to two 40-mm grenades for his M-203, and he knew he'd be needing some additional firepower for when he hit the landing site and faced the rest of Bannon's troops.

The Executioner moved through the wreckage near the courthouse, hoping to find what he needed. Among the slaughter, Bolan discovered two men in brown uniforms and one with a star pinned to his chest, which had to be Maulin. Their faces had been blown off at point-blank range, more of Bannon's work.

A hard search yielded what Bolan wanted. Picking up the two LAW rockets, he swiftly headed back through the town.

Midway down the street, he heard an enraged townsman bellow at him, "What about us? What about our town?"

Bolan gave the guy a look but kept moving, heading toward Denton's Jeep.

WITH THE COLD WIND lashing his face through the shattered windshield, Bannon replaced the radio mike. He gave Peterson a hard look. "They've landed. I'm putting ten men at the end of the trail. They're ordered to fight to the last man to make sure we get airborne."

Peterson was breathing hard, his teeth clenched, the rage clearly visible in his eyes as he guided the Jeep Cherokee down the dark highway.

"Dammit, Bannon, we lost a lot of good men back there. A lot of friends."

Bannon got busy reloading the MM-1. "What are you saying, Peterson? It bothers you, cops killing cops?"

"No. Not that." He hit the steering wheel with his palm. "That Fed, I'm sure he survived. He'll be on our ass, you can bet. If it weren't for that damn guy, we'd be at the front gates of the White House right now."

"We're still going. It's far from being over. Are you with me, soldier?"

"I'm with you."

Bannon checked behind them. Three vehicles full of the soldiers who had survived the showdown in Honor were right on their tail. He didn't even want to know how many men he'd lost, or if he'd left any wounded behind. Somehow, it had spun out of control, but there was no turning back now, no giving up to the cops. The only thing was to carry on with the original game plan.

"We'll be out of here in less than twenty minutes. Our mission is still a go," Bannon said. "I'm going to have to rearrange some of the logistics, but we're going to make it."

"You're damn right we're going to make it. We haven't come this far to fail now," Peterson agreed.

About a mile ahead, Bannon saw the flashing lights of a roadblock.

Peterson cursed.

"Get to about fifty yards of them," Bannon ordered. "Slow it down now."

He gripped the MM-1 in one fist, his other hand on the doorknob.

He felt the vehicle slow, saw the troopers with their guns already drawn, taking cover behind their cruisers.

The lives of those cops, Bannon thought, were about to change forever. What *he* had to do was larger and far more important than the lives of any man on any side of the law.

When Peterson had reached the fifty-yard mark, Bannon charged out of the Jeep and began firing the MM-1.

BOLAN CLIMBED OUT of the vehicle. His eyes took in the brilliant flames of the new kill zone as he moved toward the demolished cruisers.

The bodies of yet more cops were strewed over the highway. They hadn't stood a chance, Bolan guessed. Side arms were no match for the high-explosive launcher at Bannon's disposal. It looked to the soldier like the ex-FBI agent had simply blown them off the highway with his MM-1. Then he'd just kept on going, like it was nothing, like the lives of those men were just something in his way.

Four cruisers with flashing lights hit long squealing slides before stopping near the Jeep.

One of the lawmen cursed at the sight of the bodies.

Bolan turned slowly to look at the lawmen Dawson had put under his command. He noted that they were armed with M-16 assault rifles.

"This Bannon is finished if I have anything to say about it," a young blond trooper snarled.

As two troopers went to search the burning wrecks, Bolan got back into the Jeep, motioning for the other lawmen to follow him.

Using the map Denton had drawn for him before he'd left Honor, Bolan estimated they were less than two miles from the landing zone.

But then he discovered they were closer than that when he spotted the armed shadows off to the side of the road in front of a dark trail, less than a mile on.

Hitting the brakes, Bolan was out of the vehicle and triggering his M-203 just as the line of shadows began splitting the night with barking muzzle-flashes.

He added another blast, hurling men and wreckage to the sky and into the woods.

But the bad die hard, Bolan knew, as Bannon's hardmen continued to rise from the smoke and fire, swinging assault rifles his way.

The Executioner poured an entire clip into the mouth of the trail, then he got back into his vehicle and raced once more into the darkness.

JUST AS HE WAS about to board his jet, Bannon froze at the sound he had become all too familiar with in the past couple of hours. The merciless chatter of an automatic weapon further confirmed that his men at the end of the trail were under attack. As the fireball boiled under the treetops, Bannon knew that Belasko was alive.

He surged into the plane's cabin, barking at the pilot to get them off the ground. All around him, he saw the sheen of panic on the faces of his men. He could tell they wanted to get out and fight, instead of risk being shot down out of the sky.

Seconds later, the aircrafts began to move. Bannon stared out across the dark field. If Belasko came racing onto the field now, armed with rocket firepower...

He shoved the thought out of his mind as the jet rolled over the grassy field.

The fear was strong enough in the cabin for Bannon to feel it like a vise clamping onto him.

BOLAN RACED the Jeep across the field, angling for the line of jets rolling down the makeshift runway. Racing dangerously over unfamiliar terrain at almost eighty miles per hour, he managed to cut the gap to Bannon's jet armada to less than a hundred feet.

As the first aircraft lifted off, Bolan hit the brakes and shot out of the vehicle, a LAW in each hand.

He drew target acquisition and triggered the rocket launcher.

There was a zigzag line of streaking flame and the warhead blew the lead jet out of the sky. The second and third jets screamed for the mountains, peeling away from the fireball that seemed to hang in the sky like the sun. They quickly outdistanced any effective range for Bolan's second rocket.

He expended the second one-shot rocket launcher, taking out the fourth craft just as it was lifting off, in a brilliant flash of rolling fire.

For long moments, as a half-dozen cruisers came screaming up behind the warrior, a miniature supernova burned over the field, showing Bolan the havoc he had wreaked. With no time to avert their course, the fifth then the sixth jets became flaming scrap as wreckage pounded into their sleek frames, spreading men and machine into countless pieces across the field.

Bolan watched helplessly as the two jets shrieked over the mountains and vanished east.

## 15

The Executioner sat in an unmarked car alongside Agent Chambers. He stared into the darkness west on Pennsylvania Avenue, then checked his watch: 0435.

It was the fourth straight night Bolan had been on an all-night surveillance with Chambers, armed with M-16s with attached M-203 grenade launchers. Other unmarked cars and vans full of armed FBI and Justice Department agents were either parked at both ends of Pennsylvania Avenue in front of the White House or were patrolling the South Lawn.

In the four days since the town of Honor had burned, the medical examiners had turned up nothing to tell Bolan he'd blown Bannon out of the sky. The Executioner *knew* Bannon was alive. Out there somewhere, chafing at the bit, the Right Hand of God's leader and his troops were close. Bolan could feel it. Tonight was the night.

The soldier surveyed the grounds. All was silent around the White House, but the President was still inside, opting to stay put and ride it out, even after he'd been thoroughly briefed by every law-enforcement agency imaginable. Security in and around the Executive Mansion had been beefed up by an army of Secret Service agents and the protected airspace around the building extended. Bolan didn't think even Bannon was suicidal enough to just plow his jets into the White House, although he wasn't going to put anything past one of the most determined men he'd faced down in some time.

What had happened back in Colorado had been all over the news, but then the Justice Department had stepped in, effectively plugging any possible leaks about Bannon's intentions to attack the White House. After sitting in on all the briefings and debriefings at the Justice Building, Bolan knew the plan was to lure Bannon in. After four days of intense aerial recon by the Air Force and the CIA, there had been no sighting of Bannon's aircraft. The state and every local police force in Virginia, West Virginia, North and South Carolina, Maryland and Pennsylvania had been alerted about Bannon. Bolan's hunch was that the men had set down in a state other than his original touchdown site in Virginia and he was going to move in by road for his grandstand play.

Bolan felt Chambers's eyes on him. He knew the agent was getting impatient for something to happen.

"He'll be here," was all Bolan said.

"If he doesn't show tonight, a lot of this security is going to be called off. The President's telling us he's beginning to feel like a prisoner. It's not that they don't believe the threat is real, but there are people who are worried about the press. If the American people believe that not even the White House is safe from attack . . ."

Chambers didn't finish his sentence, but Bolan knew exactly what the agent meant.

"I appreciate all you did for me back in Colorado," Bolan told him.

A weary smile cut the man's face. "You mean for keeping you out of the news? Well, that was straight from Brognola. I'm just sorry I couldn't keep the state police from tracking you back to Honor. Maybe then we wouldn't have been looking at more than a dozen dead Colorado state troopers. When they showed up at that diner, man, you want to talk about some angry cops. By the way, you asked me to check on

Captain Dawson. He'll make it. So will the other trooper."

Bolan felt heartened at that news. Still, too many good men had died because of Bannon.

Suddenly the soldier heard the distant thunder of explosions. The radio cracked with a frantic voice telling Chambers that explosions had just gone off at the foot of the Capitol Building and somewhere on Constitution Avenue.

There were more peals of far-off thunder.

Then Bolan saw them.

Four vehicles, two vans and two trucks, raced out of the blackness west on Pennsylvania Avenue.

Bolan was out of the car and triggering his M-16 as soon as the shadows hit the walk in front of the wrought-iron gates.

Just like that, the White House was under attack. The Executioner had expected nothing less from Bannon.

Without missing a beat, Bolan, Chambers and two dozen agents of the FBI and Justice Department dropped soldiers of the Right Hand of God with rounds from grenade launchers as soon as they hit the walk.

Bolan pumped out two 40-mm hellbombs, pulverizing two of the enemy's vehicles and hammering twisted wreckage through the White House gate.

For eternal moments, the night was torn apart by the relentless din of weapons' fire and men screaming in agony.

The Executioner closed in on the killing ground, his M-16 flaming and stuttering, dropping targets all over the walk, while other hardmen were pinned to the gates by the ceaseless waves of lead delivered by the FBI and Justice agents.

Still, the enemy managed to trigger their rockets. It had been Bannon's goal all along, Bolan knew, to make his mark and carve his sick niche in history. Angling across the street and firing a relentless stream of autofire, Bolan saw the hate soldiers' rockets streak across the front lawn. One blast scythed through a line of figures racing for the gates. Secret Service agents were launched toward the White House on two, then three screaming fireballs. Another missile took a zigzag flight toward the Executive Mansion, but missed, streaking over the roof of the second story, to vanish somewhere beyond before Bolan heard the distant blast.

Then, in the firelight of burning wreckage, the soldier's gaze locked onto the face of hate he had become so familiar with.

With his MM-1 clutched in his hand, Bannon stood on the walk as bullets screamed around him, dropping his soldiers.

Bolan fired his M-16, but Bannon was already darting for one of his vans. Still, the Executioner's line of 5.56-mm lead managed to march up his enemy's side, hurling him to the street.

Bannon struggled to stand.

The soldier stopped in the middle of Pennsylvania Avenue, about a dozen yards from Bannon, and held his ground.

All around the warrior shadows were spinning and dropping in the murderous firefight as FBI and Justice agents chased down the surviving soldiers of the Right Hand of God.

Bannon grabbed his MM-1, his blood soaking his clothing.

With a steady hand, Bolan drew target acquisition on his enemy's chest. With the thought that he was a heartbeat away from making the world a better place in which to live, the Executioner triggered the M-203 and gave the night one final roar of death.

Killer rays from space threaten
to cook America's goose....

# THE Destroyer

## #105 Scorched Earth

### Created by
### WARREN MURPHY
### and RICHARD SAPIR

A single superheated zap from an invisible object in space
literally vaporizes the Biobubble habitat scientists. More
sizzling attacks are followed by eyewitness sightings of
giant Cyrillic letters in the sky.

Look for it in December, wherever Gold Eagle books are sold.

**Don't miss out on the action in these titles featuring
THE EXECUTIONER® and STONY MAN™!**

The Red Dragon Trilogy

| #64210 | FIRE LASH | $3.75 U.S. | ☐ |
| | | $4.25 CAN. | ☐ |
| #64211 | STEEL CLAWS | $3.75 U.S. | ☐ |
| | | $4.25 CAN. | ☐ |
| #64212 | RIDE THE BEAST | $3.75 U.S. | ☐ |
| | | $4.25 CAN. | ☐ |

Stony Man™

| #61903 | NUCLEAR NIGHTMARE | $4.99 U.S. | ☐ |
| | | $5.50 CAN. | ☐ |
| #61904 | TERMS OF SURVIVAL | $4.99 U.S. | ☐ |
| | | $5.50 CAN. | ☐ |
| #61905 | SATAN'S THRUST | $4.99 U.S. | ☐ |
| | | $5.50 CAN. | ☐ |
| #61906 | SUNFLASH | $5.50 U.S. | ☐ |
| | | $6.50 CAN. | ☐ |
| #61907 | THE PERISHING GAME | $5.50 U.S. | ☐ |
| | | $6.50 CAN. | ☐ |

(limited quantities available on certain titles)

| **TOTAL AMOUNT** | $ |
| **POSTAGE & HANDLING** | $ |
| ($1.00 for one book, 50¢ for each additional) | |
| **APPLICABLE TAXES*** | $_____ |
| **TOTAL PAYABLE** | $_____ |
| (check or money order—please do not send cash) | |

To order, complete this form and send it, along with a check or money order for the total above, payable to Gold Eagle Books, to: **In the U.S.:** 3010 Walden Avenue, P.O. Box 9077, Buffalo, NY 14269-9077; **In Canada:** P.O. Box 636, Fort Erie, Ontario, L2A 5X3.

Name:_____

Address:_____ City:_____

State/Prov.:_____ Zip/Postal Code:_____

*New York residents remit applicable sales taxes.
 Canadian residents remit applicable GST and provincial taxes.

GEBACK16